"Dance with me."

Max slides his arm around my waist and leads me to the periphery of the dance floor. Then he spins me around and the music catches me in its groove. My dancing is sure and light, and I move further and further away from the problems—at least for tonight....

He takes my hand and gives me a little twirl.

When I face him again, my head is spinning and that big, white full moon that rose so gracefully over the river suddenly has a twin. I blink several times until the two moons merge back into one.

I don't know if it's because of the beer or the dancing or the loud music, but I like the rush. I haven't felt the likes of this since...well, in far too long. Unencumbered by past grief and the uncertainty of the future.

I'm free.

I want to stay frozen in this moment when everything is safe and fresh and new....

Nancy Robards Thompson

Award-winning author Nancy Robards Thompson is a
sister, wife and mother who has lived the majority of her
life south of the Mason-Dixon line. As the oldest sibling,
she reveled in her ability to make her brother laugh at
inappropriate moments and soon learned she could get
away with it by proclaiming, "What? I wasn't doing
anything." It's no wonder that upon graduating from
college with a degree in journalism, she discovered that
reporting "just the facts" bored her silly. Since she hung
up her press pass to write novels full-time, critics have
deemed her books "funny, smart and observant." She
loves chocolate, champagne, cats and art (though not
necessarily in that order). When she's not writing, she
enjoys spending time with her family, reading, hiking and
doing yoga.

BEAUTY SHOP
TALES

Nancy Robards Thompson

BEAUTY SHOP TALES

copyright © 2007 by Nancy Robards Thompson

i s b n - 1 3 : 9 7 8 - 0 - 3 7 3 - 8 8 1 4 2 - 0

i s b n - 1 0 :   0 - 3 7 3 - 8 8 1 4 2 - 8

TheNextNovel.com

 HARLEQUIN®

PRINTED IN U.S.A.

From the Author

Dear Reader,

Many of us have heard the Alexander Pope quote "To err is human, to forgive divine." It's a good thought, but sometimes we're more human than divine.

Such is the case in *Beauty Shop Tales*, when Avril Carson discovers her best friend, Kally, has betrayed her in the worst way a friend could. Avril has to search deep inside to find the means to forgive. As she does, a funny thing happens—she learns to love in ways she never thought possible.

You might say it took a village (or at least a writing community) to bring Avril and Kally's journey to life. Bits and pieces of the story had been brewing for some time. I knew I wanted to explore the limits of friendship and the healing power of forgiveness, set against the intimate and sometimes smothering backdrop of small-town life. Still, it didn't quite gel until my writing buddies and I went on a plotting retreat and pieced it all together. It was a fun time. Like Avril and Kally's story, the perfect illustration of how friendship can sometimes move mountains and accomplish what, at first glance, seems impossible.

Enjoy!

Nancy Robards Thompson

This book is dedicated to the midwives of this story—
Kathleen O'Brien, Ann Bair, Lori Harris,
Terry Backhus and Teresa Elliott Brown.
And to Larri Mattison, who kept nudging me
to write a book set in a salon.
Special thanks to Tammy Strickland and Pam and
Bill LaBud for educating me on leukemia.
Love and appreciation to my critique partners
Catherine Kean and Elizabeth Grainger.
As always, Michael and Jen—*Je vous aime beaucoup*.

CHAPTER 1

The Garden of Proserpine

Here, where the world is quiet,
Here, where all trouble seems
Dead winds and spent waves riot
In doubtful dreams of dreams;
I watch the green field growing
For reaping folk and sowing,
For harvest-time and mowing,
A sleepy world of streams.

—Algernon Charles Swinburne

Today, as I fly out of LAX, probably for the last time, the souvenirs I'm taking with me are two truths I gleaned doing hair in the Hollywood movie industry: 1) appearance is everything; and 2) reality, that eternal shape-shifter, is the biggest illusion of all.

Reality is 99.9 percent perception. It morphs into whatever form best moves ahead the perceiver.

As I, Avril Carson, thirty-five-year-old widow of Chet, and *former* aspiring-starlet-turned-Hollywood-stylist, wipe my clammy palms on my Dolce & Gabbanas—which I bought gently worn at a consignment shop for a fraction of the retail price...but no one needs to know that—and prepare to speed into the wild blue yonder into the next chapter of my life, witness Hollywood truths one and two play out in real life.

It goes like this: Even though I loathe flying, I've convinced myself that I *must* fly across country because the alternative is to come rolling back home into Sago Beach, Florida, in a Greyhound bus.

No can do. Ride the bus, that is.

Not when these jeans retail for nearly three times the cost of a bus ticket.

Not when I'd have to travel twenty-seven hundred miles, stopping at forty-one different stations along the way, to arrive at 3:42 in the morning. Call me vain, but I refuse to go two days, sixteen hours and fifteen minutes without a shower. It makes my skin crawl just thinking about it and the mélange of aromas simmering in that busload of unwashed strangers.

If personal hygiene is too selfish to justify bus snobbery, think of my mother. She has taken such pleasure in my being the hometown girl who's made good in Hollywood; I simply can't let her down by arriving in less than style.

Work with me, here. I mean, come on, I *hate* to fly. If I were being completely real, I'd keep my feet on the ground and take that bus—body odor be damned—over hurling through the air from one coast to the other.

But it's not an option. So, I keep reminding myself of the above rationale and that flying is safer than traveling cross-country via ground transportation. *Blah, blah, blah—*

Full of Dramamine, which has not yet kicked in, I board the plane, settle into my aisle seat and try to center myself.

Oh, God… I'm *really* doing this.

Chet would've been proud of me for venturing so far out of my comfort zone. I press my leg against my carry-on, which holds the box of his ashes, hoping to absorb some of his courage.

Chet Marcus Carson, extreme sports reporter for WKGM Hollywood. Nothing scared him, which is part of the reason he's dead…nine months now. Parasailing accident.

Chet Marcus Carson, the reason I ended up in Hollywood to pursue my dream. Much to my mother's hysterical dismay, he yanked me up out of Sago Beach—population 212—and set me firmly on the road to making something of myself. I was going to be an actress. A star. Just like all my favorites in the old black-and-white romances. The ones I used to watch over and over again. The ones that made me dream big and believe in happily ever after.

And Chet, he was going to be a sportscaster. Together we

were going to set the world on fire and never look back at the Podunk town of our youth.

God, that sounds so stupid now. So naive.

I suppose I was. And now, Chet Marcus Carson is the reason I'm going home. I tried my best to stick it out on my own, but by the time I lost Chet, the Hurray-For-Holly-wood, rose-colored glasses were gone; I wasn't cut out to be an actress—not in this how-bad-do-you-want-it, bare-it-all day and age.

My dream was over, but Chet's rose like a turbo-inflated hot air balloon. I resorted to the only things I knew: doing hair and being a strong support system for him. Through his contacts, he got me a few jobs doing hair on the sets of various local productions, but my heart wasn't in it. Once I got a look behind the curtain and glimpsed the real Holly-wood, all I wanted was to ground myself in reality. I wanted to raise a family, to be a good wife—to be normal again.

Then one day it all came crashing down. The only man I'd ever loved was dead. And I was stuck in this soulless town that was just one big reminder that somehow I had to go on without him.

But how?

How in the world could I do that?

Still, today, I'm only supposed to think positive thoughts.

Buckling myself into this Boeing 707, I glance at the woman in the window seat, sitting all snug and relaxed, listening to her iPod, shutting out the rest of the world. Taking a cue from her, I focus on my breathing and try to redirect my thoughts to a happy place, but before I get there, a man pauses in the aisle beside me.

"Excuse me, I think I'm sitting next to you." He removes a black cowboy hat, glances at his boarding pass and gestures to the vacant middle seat. "Row twenty-five? Seat B?"

The guy is tall—maybe six-four. The manly-man variety that takes up lots of space. The type who sprawls and hogs both armrests.

Great.

My legs feel like overcooked bucatini, but somehow, I manage to stand without whacking my head on the low-flying overhead storage bin.

The cowboy can't back up because there's a long line of people behind him. Behind me, an older couple is stashing their belongings. With no other options, the cowboy and I do an awkward dance as he slides past me to the middle seat.

Soon enough, I'm settled and attempting to resume my stream of reassuring thoughts. Let's see, where was I...?

Aerodynamics. Uhh, sure...that's as good a place as any to start.

Aerodynamics is a *proven* reality, not just Hollywood hype. Aerodynamics allow this *eight-hundred-and-seventy-thousand-pound* tin can, which is comprised of six million parts and one hundred and forty-seven thousand pounds of "high-strength aluminum," to defy gravity.

Which seems utterly ridiculous if you consider the laws of gravity. Because something this heavy is not supposed to fly. Then the airline fills it full of people and overstuffed luggage and those tiny bottles of booze and—

Oh, God…

I feel as if someone's slipped a noose around my neck. Perhaps I need that booze to preempt an anxiety attack.

All right. Settle down. Breathe.

Aerodynamics.

I learned those factoids about the makeup of an airplane on the Boeing Web site when I was surfing for comforting facts to quell my fears. I thought if anyone could sing the praises of flight safety, the airline manufacturer would have the shtick down pat.

They did.

Still, knowing myself like I do, I came up with a backup plan. Thus was born my list of the drawbacks of bus travel.

And you thought I was an insufferable snob, didn't you?

I have one word for you: Self-preservation.

Let's just get through this. Focus, Avril. Happy thoughts.

At this point, the flight attendants are midway through their pretakeoff spiel.

"Ladies and gentlemen, please take note of the emergency exits located throughout the cabin." They point their manicured fingers toward the sides of the plane and smile like we're all at Disneyland. "In the unlikely event of an emergency, lights along the floor will direct you to an exit…."

Emergency.

The engines fire up.

Oh, God… The noose tightens.

I am perfectly safe.

People fly every day.

Statistically, I have a better chance of winning the lottery than being killed in a plane crash. Hollywood cannot change that reality.

Oh, God…

As the engines roar, and the plane taxis down the runway, I'm gripped by the third Hollywood truth: When bullshit fails, backpedal like hell and disassociate yourself from the lie as fast as you can.

I hate to fly. I really, really hate it. I can't believe I tried to make myself buy into this crap. Forget aerodynamics. Huge, phallic-shaped metal objects that weigh hundreds of thousands of pounds are not supposed to swim weightlessly through the air thirty-five thousand feet above the clouds and the earth.

The words *Let me out of this death trap!* gurgle up in my throat, but even if I could find my voice, it's too late. The plane lifts off. The G-forces press me into the seat like invisible hands hell-bent on pinning me down.

I hug myself and squeeze my eyes shut. My breath comes in short, quick gasps.

"Oh, God. Oh, God. Oh, God. Oh, God!"

"Are you okay?" the cowboy asks.

I nod, vigorously, and realize I was probably muttering *Oh, God* under my breath. I hope I didn't sound like I was having an orgasm.

Biting the inside of my cheeks to keep other words from flying out, I draw in another deep breath through my nose. Come to think of it, I hate the smell of planes—that blend of humans, jet fuel and airplane food—almost as much as bus odor. Still, the scent, pleasant or not, is a touchstone, an anchor to the here and now, and I latch onto it like a life preserver, hugging myself tighter.

"Takeoff's my favorite part of the flight."

Huh?

I open one eye and look at the cowboy. Not only is he taking up both armrests, he's listing in my direction.

He's so much bigger than Chet, who was lean and fair and Hollywood fabulous. The cowboy is dark and good-looking if you like a raven-eyed, five-o'clock-shadow, feral-looking, Tim-McGraw sort of man. I shift away from his manliness.

"There's always so much possibility when a plane takes off." He has one of those piercing, look-you-in-the-eyes kind of gazes. "It's so symbolic. New places. New beginnings. New opportunities. What's your favorite part of the ride?"

My favorite—? Why is he talking to me? "I hate to fly."

"Really." The word is a statement laced with a hint of sarcasm. "How can anybody hate to fly? Think of all you'd miss letting fear rule your life."

Who in the hell does he think he is? Anthony Robbins?

"I'm here, aren't I? I'm certainly not letting fear rule me. Otherwise I'd have my feet planted firmly on the ground rather than hanging out up here in the clouds, thirty-five thousand feet above—"

The plane dips into an air pocket.

"Oh, God!"

The words are a whimper, and I melt into my seat, too scared to be thoroughly mortified for being such a big baby.

Okay, maybe I'm a little mortified. Because he's still staring at me.

Oh, leave me alone. I close my eyes again, feeling the first waves of the Dramamine. That foggy, far-off haziness that clouds the head before it closes the eyes is creeping up on me.

"Okay, you get partial credit for being here," says the wise guy.

Partial credit? Like I care. I swallow a yawn.

"But to get full credit, you have to tell me your favorite part of the flight."

I'm tempted to tell him where to put his favorite part. To leave me alone so I can go to sleep and wake up when we're safely back on the ground. But this guy is persistent. It'll be a long, uncomfortable flight if I piss him off. I revert to

Hollywood truth number four: Tell them what they want to hear and they'll go away.

"My favorite part of the flight?"

He nods.

My mouth is dry, but I manage to say, "When they open the door at the gate. Now leave me alone so I can go to sleep. My Dramamine is kicking in."

"Come on," he says. "You can do better than that."

"Excuse me?"

"That's a cop-out. Opening the door at the gate is not part of the flight. The flight's over."

"Well, it's certainly better than the take off—"

I gesture at the air to indicate the turbulent departure, only to realize we've leveled off and are cruising at that smooth, steady pace that's almost bearable.

He smiles and takes the in-flight magazine out of the seat pocket. "Sleep well."

MIRACULOUSLY, I do manage to sleep most of the nonstop flight. My eyes flutter open to the sound of the flight attendant's announcement asking everyone to secure their tray tables and return their seats to the upright position as we prepare to land in Orlando.

I stretch and rub my stiff neck.

"See, that wasn't so bad, was it?" says the cowboy.

"It's not over yet."

Vaguely wondering what a guy like him was doing in L.A., I retrieve my purse from under the seat, pull out my Lancôme Dual Finish compact and the red lipstick I got in the free gift when I purchased the powder. Something to distract me while we get this last part of the journey over with.

Out of the corner of my eye, I see him watching me primp.

"Are you visiting Orlando or coming home?"

"Neither." I blot my lips and check the mirror to make sure my lipstick is on straight. "I'm from a small town over on the east coast."

"Cocoa Beach?"

I shake my head. "Sago Beach."

He nods. "It's pretty over there. Visiting family?"

I snap the compact shut, drop the cosmetics into my purse and look him square in the eyes, ready to give him the polite brush-off. Only then do I realize just how cute this guy is. Nice face. So totally not my type.

For a split second, I hope I didn't do something repulsive while I slept, like drool, or snort, or sit there with my mouth gaping open.

I could only do things like that around Chet. My foot finds the bag with his ashes, and I blink away the thought. It doesn't matter how I appeared to the cowboy while I was sleeping. Rubbing the place where my wedding ring should've been with my thumb, I say, "I'm moving back."

"Welcome home."

"Thank you."

Home. *Hmm.* I suppose Sago Beach has always been home, even when I was away.

Hollywood certainly never was.

It was something I had to get out of my system—like a bad boyfriend who treated me unkindly and sent me running back to my mother. Only this bad relationship lasted seventeen years and cost me my husband and my youth. Chet was really the one who wanted to live there because it was good for our careers. But come to find out, I can take my career anywhere. Just like now that I'm bringing it back home to my mother's salon.

"The name's Max Wright." He extends a hand. I shake it. "What's yours?"

"Avril."

The plane hits another air pocket. I grope for the armrests. In my panic, I end up grabbing his arm and releasing it as if it burns.

"Sorry."

He smiles, a little half smile, and I like the way the outer corners of his eyes tilt down. "Just relax, Avril. The worst part is over."

Hollywood truths one and two kick in and I want to believe him.

Yeah, now that I'm home the worst is just about over.

I believe that for about fifteen minutes—until we deplane and make our way to baggage claim, where my mother and half the population of Sago Beach are standing under a banner that proclaims Welcome home, Avril!! Sago Beach's very own beauty operator to the stars.

CHAPTER 2

I want to die.

Truly, I do.

Because I hate surprises. My mother knows it. Still, once she gets an idea in that red head of hers, she tends to forget everything outside the scope of her plan.

The surprise banner-flying airport welcoming committee—a collection of at least twenty of Sago Beach's finest—has my mother's name written all over it.

The scene unfolds as the escalator carries me from the main terminal down to baggage claim, and I reconcile that, ready or not, this is small-town life. It's nothing like Hollywood, where you're invisible unless you're the It Girl of the Moment.

I have two choices: I can either turn and hightail it back up the escalator, or suck it up and greet them like a decent person. It only takes a split second to decide that despite the embarrassment factor of seeing my name along with the words *Sago Beach's very own beauty operator to the stars*, emblazoned in bright letters on a long sheet of brown craft paper, I'm touched that these people would take the time to make a banner, much less come all the way to Orlando—a good hour's drive from the coast—to make me feel welcome.

Ready or not, I'm home.

"All this is for you?" Max smiles and a dimple winks at me from his left cheek.

I hitch the tote with Chet's ashes upon my shoulder, feeling oddly sheepish and a little unfaithful that all of them will see a strange man talking to me.

"Beauty operator to the stars, huh?" He whistles. "I didn't realize I was sitting next to royalty."

"They're good people," I say, suddenly protective of the folks, who, just a moment ago, embarrassed the living daylights out of me.

"I can see that. They're really glad you're back."

The escalator reaches the bottom, delivering us to the baggage claim, and my friends and family surge forward.

"Nice to meet you, princess," he says.

Princess? Normally, I'd spit out a snappy retort, but with my welcoming committee rallying around me, I don't want to encourage any further conversation with Max. That would only lead to questions from the fine people of Sago Beach. Especially Mama.

I do the next best thing. I pretend I didn't hear him as everyone envelopes me.

Mama is at the helm, of course, hugging me first. Her hair is the same rusty-carrot shade that it's been for as far back as I can remember. It's long and big, as if Dolly Parton had a run-in with a vat of V8 juice. She's a beautiful sight, and I feel so safe in her slight arms that I want to cry.

There's Justine Wittage and Carolyn Hayward, Mama's longtime customers, Bucky Farley and Tim Dennison, among others in the crowd, who hug and kiss me and say, "Oh, darlin' ain't you a sight?"

My old friend Kally is conspicuously absent from the fray. It gives me a little pang that she didn't come, but we haven't exactly been on good terms the past five years or so.

"I suppose you're too good for us now that you've been hobnobbing with them movie stars?" Marjorie Cooper, Sago Beach's token busybody, smiles her wonderful gap-toothed smile.

"Of course not, Margie, I'm still the same girl you've always known."

"I know ya are, hon. I'm just yanking your chain." She enfolds me in a hug that threatens to squeeze the stuffing out of me. "It's so good to have you home."

Finally, after everyone has a chance to say hello, they decide to head for home.

"No sense in you all standing around and waiting for the baggage," Mama insists. "Y'all go on back home."

This incites another round of hugs and welcome-homes and I feel a twinge of guilt that they all made the two-hour round-trip for less than five minutes of togetherness.

"We'll see you soon," says Bucky Farley, who has lingered behind the rest of them.

"Bucky, you go on now and get out of here. We'll manage just fine."

Mama growls the words like a tiger. I wonder what's got her back up all of a sudden. For a split second, I wonder if she's going to object to any and all men who show interest in me. Not that I'm interested in dating Bucky. He's not my type at all—not quite old enough to be my father, more like an uncle.

If there's one thing I don't need it's my mother screening my friends. But she loved Chet. We'd been a couple so long, we were like one person. It would take everyone a while to get used to me being on my own.

Mama links her arm through mine as we move to carousel number four to get my bags. I glance up and see Max standing alone across the way. He smiles and tips his hat.

"Who is that?" Mama blurts.

I shrug nonchalantly, looking everywhere but in his direction. "He sat next to me on the plane."

"Handsome."

"Really? I hadn't noticed."

"He certainly noticed you. Look at him staring." So much for the Bucky Farley theory. "Did you give him your number?"

"Mother."

"Well, he certainly is nice-looking—"

"Stop it."

"Avril, honey, I know you loved Chet. We all loved him, but you're a young woman. There's no harm in giving a good-looking guy your phone number."

I haven't even been home for a full hour and already she's pushing my buttons.

"He didn't ask for my number. Okay? Besides, I don't have to hook up with the first guy who's nice to me."

"I didn't suggest anything of the sort. But you've got to start somewhere and well, why not go for one with looks?"

One of my bags pops out of the chute and I retrieve it with hopes this interruption will preempt further discussion about the cowboy. I don't want to argue with my mother on my first day back. Now that I'm home, I'll have the rest of my life to do that.

When I turn to haul the big, black bag over to her so she can watch it while I collect the rest of my things, she's not there. I make a slow circle until I finally spot her on the other side of baggage claim talking to Max, pen and paper in hand.

"IF HE WANTED MY telephone number, he would've asked *me* for it." I feel murderous as I heft my bags into the trunk of Mama's pristine 1955, cherry-red T-Bird, which she's parked catty-corner across two spaces in the airport garage.

It's on the tip of my tongue to tell her parking like this is begging someone to key the gleaming paint, but when I turn around, she's standing there watching me with her arms akimbo, one hip jutting out, an undaunted smile on her face.

Vintage Tess Mulligan.

"Oh, don't get your panties in a wad, baby. Do you really think I'd give your phone number to a total stranger—even if he was a tall hunk of handsome man? Even if the number I'd be giving out is *my* phone number? Hmm. Maybe I *should've* given him the number." She mutters this last part under her breath and I want to tell her to go for it, to knock herself out.

I love my mother. We're close, despite her ability to drive a stuffed elephant up the wall. If I'm completely honest, I suppose the things I do don't make sense to her. It's one of those weird codependent relationships.

I can get mad at her, but if anyone else uttered a cross word about her, they'd have to deal with me. And it wouldn't be pretty.

When I lived in California, the miles between us helped. She flew out to see me about four times a year—and about every two months since I lost Chet—because of my fear of flying. In fact, I haven't been home in years since she was so good about coming out to visit.

The distance was our friend. When she meddled, I could curtail the phone conversation, and the next time we talked she'd be on to something else.

The staccato honk of someone locking a vehicle echoes

in the garage and a car *whooshes* by belching a plume of exhaust as the driver accelerates.

Mama brandishes a cream-colored business card like a magician making a coin appear from thin air. "I got *his* number for you. The ball is in your court, missy. *You've* gotta call *him*."

"I'm *not* calling him." I spit the words like darts over the top of the car, but she ducks and slides into the driver's seat.

I slam the trunk and fume for a few seconds.

Why did I think she'd give me even a short grace period before she started her antics? It'll be a small miracle if we don't kill each other living under the same roof and working in the same salon—even if it's only for the interim.

Moisture beads on my forehead, my upper lip, the small of my back. It's warm for February—but that's Florida for you—and my Dolce & Gabbanas suddenly feel like suffocating plastic wrap.

I don't need someone collecting business cards for me. I can get my own dates. If and when I'm ready to do so.

Feeling trapped inside the four walls of *chez* Tess Mulligan—well, her car, anyway—*finding a place of my own* leaps to the top of my mental priority list.

Mama cranks the engine, and I open the car door and buckle myself in for a bumpy ride.

As she slips the gearshift into Reverse, her nails, the same red as her car, click on the metal shaft. Then she stretches her right arm over the seatback. Her compact little body lists toward me as she looks over her shoulder before cranking the wheel with her left hand and maneuvering the car out of the parking spaces.

In the graying garage light, I see the deep etchings time has sketched on her face. They seem more pronounced, shadowed, in this half light. At this angle, the crepey skin of her throat looks loose and paper-thin. In this quiet moment, I see beneath the bold, brassiness of her facade down to the heart and soul. She looks older, mortal, vulnerable. Funny, how these things go unnoticed during the daily razzmatazz of the Tess Mulligan show—until the camera fades and the lights go down and she's not performing for an audience.

I swallow the harsh words sizzling in my mouth and wash them down with a little compassion. Even though the zingers stick in my throat, I turn the subject to a more amiable topic.

"How's Kally?"

Mama's jaw tightens. She shifts forward on the seat, her posture rod-straight, and shrugs.

Kally and I have known each other since we were in diapers. Once, she was my best friend in the world. Chet's, too. In fact, she and this guy, Jake Brumly, and Chet and I used to be known as the fearsome foursome in high school.

Then we grew up.

She and Jake broke up. Chet and I got married and moved away. I'd like to say life just got in the way, but it's not that simple. In fact, it got downright ugly—all because of money.

It's awful. It really is.

About four or five years ago, Chet told her we'd invest in this business of hers, this artsy—or so I've heard, I've never seen it—coffee shop called Lady Marmalade's. As much as we both adored Kally and as much as Chet wanted everyone back home to believe we were living the beautiful life in L.A., we didn't have that kind of extra cash. I had to be the heavy and say no.

She got mad when we pulled out. Just like that. Can you imagine?

Then she had a kid and our paths sort of forked off in two different directions before we could make amends.

I suppose I didn't help matters.

I'll admit it, I was a little jealous when she got pregnant. Okay, I was *a lot* jealous because she had the one thing I desperately wanted and couldn't have. A baby.

I would've traded all the Hollywood glitz and glam, all the movies I worked on, all the parties and elbow-rubbing with the stars for one precious little baby.

But when you're infertile, all the bargaining in the world doesn't make a difference.

And Kally wasn't even married. Still isn't as far as I know. If you don't think *that* raised a few Sago Beach brows?

Mama is still ticked at Kally. Not because she had a baby out of wedlock. Because come to find out, even after I put my foot down about not lending her the money, Chet went behind my back and funded her business. In the aftermath of his death, I discovered Chet had a checking account I knew nothing about. Through it, I followed a messy paper trail of canceled checks made out to Kally. He was funneling her the money that was supposed to go into our 401K. Four freakin' years of this. I had no idea the money wasn't going where it was supposed to go. Chet was the financier of our relationship, paid the bills, set the budget—which is why I was flabbergasted when he suggested we invest in Kally's business. He knew better than I that we didn't have the extra cash.

This is not a good thing to uncover just weeks after your husband dies. This secret felt like I'd discovered they were having an affair—thank God for that twenty-seven-hundred-mile chastity belt. Or I might have suspected something, which was stupid because in all the years we'd known each other, never ever did I pick up one iota of a vibe that they might be interested in a little hanky panky.

It was too much to handle all at once, these two disasters. It's not like I could get answers from Chet, and Kally was pretty tightlipped when I asked her to explain.

Mama went totally ballistic. She called up Kally, read her the riot act and asked her how she could take that money from us? I suppose she felt Kally had betrayed her by virtue of betraying me and took it doubly hard because Kally had always been like another daughter to her. Especially after Kally's mother, Caro, passed away, gosh…not too long before Chet started giving Kally the money.

Mama went off, insisting Kally give me a stake in Lady Marmalade's since the money that kept the place afloat should've gone to take care of me after my husband's death.

For the record, I want nothing to do with that coffee shop. As far as I'm concerned, I'll go five miles out of my way to avoid it, which might not be so hard since she chose to set up shop over in Cocoa Beach.

I've had months to make my peace with the situation. And I have, for the most part. Really.

Kally and I haven't talked. But I'm at peace. Which is a good thing since I'm bound to run in to her now that I'm back.

All I know is if Kally Fuller could take the money and still look at herself in the mirror— Well, I suppose she's ventured farther down that divergent path than I realized she was capable.

As my mother nears the line of tollbooths, she grabs her purse and roots around in it, alternately looking down at her lap and back at the road.

"Here, Mama, let me pay for this. How much is it?" I unbuckle my purse for my wallet.

She pulls out a twenty and waves me off. "I got it."

"I wish you'd at least let me pay the toll. You drove all the way over here to get me—"

"I'm your mother. Of course I'd do that. You just hush." She rolls down her window and hands the toll-taker the money.

I sink into my seat, twelve years old again, my mother running the show.

CHAPTER 3

I'd forgotten how pretty natural Florida is this time of year. When the cycle of afternoon rains cooperate and show up on schedule, everything is lush and green and tropical. Crepe Myrtles, hibiscus and oleanders dot the highway in a kaleidoscope of color.

The scenery washes over me like a soothing bath as the black ribbon of flat Florida highway slices through the landscape, eventually reaching the subtropical marshlands that bridge the city to the coast.

Silent rivers of grass succumb to a watery wilderness of cabbage palms, cypress trees and teardrop-shaped hammock islands, formed of their own decomposing selves gradually accumulating over thousands of years.

In the middle of the slough, a great white heron spreads its wings as an ibis searches the shallows, against a brilliant backdrop of devastatingly blue, late-afternoon sky. If Monet had painted Florida, this could be his canvas.

For some reason the scene reminds me of the story of Persephone. I wasn't familiar with Greek myth until I moved to Hollywood. I'd never really studied the classics, but I did hair on the movie *Persephone;* the scenery we're passing now reminds me of how Hades, the god of the underworld, broke through the earth in his chariot, grabbed Persephone and carried her back to hell.

I imagine the place where Hades entered was similar to this. I half expect him to come crashing through and drag me back to L.A. Funny, in a roundabout, convoluted way, Mama could've likened Chet to Hades, swooping me off to Hollywood far away from her.

I glance at my mother, who looks content as she quietly drives me home. She smiles at me and turns on some music. Patsy Cline's "Crazy" drifts from the CD player and Mama sings the part, "Crazy for feelin' so blue…" Her rich alto veering into a velvety harmony.

I suppose, like Persephone, the urge to go home has niggled at me for a while. I just had to get over feeling like going home to Sago Beach meant I'd failed. I mean coming home again after all these years without a whole lot to show for myself—my dream of acting didn't exactly pan out, I'm childless and my husband died.

But that's not really failure. Not like three strikes and you're out. Is it? Because I tried. I *really* tried to do it on my own. Honestly, it's taken me this long to come to terms with the fact that I'm a widow.

A *widow.*

DOWNTOWN SAGO BEACH consists of one long, bricked street stretching through the center of the tiny town like a makeshift movie set.

Main Street runs parallel and two roads west of A1A, which fronts the beach. I've always liked how downtown is set apart from the beach-going day-trippers. Still, enough of them find their way over to support the Sago Beach businesses, but since there are no hotels and the town rolls up its welcome mat at five-thirty, they all go back over to Cocoa Beach or the other more touristy destinations for the night.

My first glimpse of home hits me like a favorite flick I'd seen over and over in my youth, but had forgotten how much I loved it. Downtowns like this don't exist anymore. Certainly not in L.A. They've been abandoned and torn down to make way for strip malls and Gallerias. But it's as though someone has waved a magic wand over downtown Sago Beach, and made time stand still—right down to the banner stretched across the road that reads: "Founder's Day Celebration and Street Dance."

It's been years since I've been home, but I recognize the banner. It's the same one they've used every year for as far back as I remember. Everything looks exactly as I last remember it—no, better. Fresher. Lovelier, despite the sameness. Much more comforting than anything since I lost Chet.

The street is lined with locally owned businesses and quaint little one-of-a-kind shops. Even the bank looks pretty and inviting, with its unique sign shaped like a palm tree and window boxes of flaming geraniums. When I left Sago Beach, I didn't realize all this prettiness was out of the ordinary. Coming home, I recognize it for the rare treasure it is, and I marvel at the wide, clean sidewalks and huge ceramic planters full of sunflowers, all turned toward the street, vying for a place in the soft, late afternoon light.

I wonder if they still change the flowers to celebrate the seasons?

Mama slows the car to a crawl and motions a car behind us to pass, to take it all in.

Oh, there's the toy store full of games and dolls, hand-crafted stick horses and model trains. My heart contracts when I think of how I used to dream of shopping there for toys for the babies Chet and I would have.

As we inch down Main Street, tears well in my eyes. I roll down the window, and breathe in a great gulp of Sago Beach—air hot as a furnace, laced with a humid, lazy brine. The essence of home. It goes straight to my head and fills my heart with eager apprehension. If *eager apprehension* is an oxymoron, well, that's exactly how I feel. Like an oxymoron.

Too young to be a widow. Too old to be on my own and back at square one in this town I left so many years ago… Still, I can't help but fall in love with it all over again. Changed in so many ways, but longing for everything to still be the same.

Oh, there's The Riviera, a clothing boutique Mama calls

"Resort-Mart." They sell crisp, expensive resort wear in garish shades of magenta, orange, chartreuse and turquoise. All you need is a little sun damage, some baby-blue, cream eye shadow and a tube of frosted coral lipstick and you, too, can look like you belong among the retired resort set.

Across the street is Paula's Bakery, which makes the world's very best Parker House rolls. At the crack of dawn on holidays the line to pick up those coveted rolls stretches down the sidewalk. Ah, and there's the Yum Yum Shop, a real old-fashioned ice-cream parlor where they still make their own ice cream in flavors like mango, chocolate-covered cherry, café latte, and lavender, in addition to the standard chocolate, vanilla, strawberry, and cookies and cream, which I swear they invented and everyone else copied. It's right next door to Joe's Hardware, with its gleaming white clapboard exterior, which is right next to the Sago Diner, which is next to… I gaze down the street, trying to catch a glimpse of the place I'd been holding my breath waiting to see…. My mother's beauty shop, Tess's Tresses, and the small apartment above it, where I grew up.

Right there on the corner— With what looks like white bed sheets drawn across the large plateglass window.

"New drapes?" I ask.

"No." She keeps her gaze pinned on the road as she accelerates into a left turn.

Okay, I can take a hint. We're not discussing the sheets

or drapes or whatever they are. I've haven't even set foot inside the salon. I'll hold off redecorating it.

She makes two more quick lefts—the first onto Broad Street, which runs behind the storefronts, then into her driveway.

Home.

"My goodness, it's nearly six o'clock. You're probably starving, aren't you?"

I hadn't really thought about food because my stomach was a little upset after the flight, but now that she mentions it… "Sure. I could eat."

"Let's get your bags in and we'll grab a bite, but first, I want to show you something real quick in the beauty shop."

It's strange walking through this portal to my adolescent sanctuary. My father died when I was five, and my mother never remarried. So it was just us girls all those years, snug in our little apartment above the salon—or beauty shop, as Mama's always called it. But we were happy, Mama and I.

Stepping inside, I squint in the dim light of the vestibule, and breathe in the familiar scent of permanent solution, fried food and Tess's perfume. It may not sound very appetizing, but it smells like my childhood.

Five paces straight ahead is the door to the beauty shop; to the left is the narrow staircase that leads up to the apartment. Exactly as always. I follow Mama upstairs safe in this bubble of sameness.

At the top of the steps, on the landing outside the door to our apartment, I stop to gaze out the single aluminum window. Its bent screen and dirty glass looks as though it hasn't been washed since I left. Still, through the haze, the deep forest leaves of the laurel oak tree that stands next to the driveway wave at me on a gust of wind. I have no idea how old that tree is, but it's huge, with roots running under the sidewalk and drive, pushing up the concrete as if to prove its dominance. Its arthritic branches stretch all the way to the house, scratching lovingly at the glass as dust motes dance in the muted light.

Beyond it, through the branches, I look down at the orange tree, in all its magnificence. It always yields an abundant crop in the cool months. Then it drops its oranges and a blanket of shade over the side yard. Beyond that, I see the houses on the street with their yard ornaments and hedges and flowerbeds, twilight settling on their rooftops, each house a vessel of continuity and similitude, no matter who lives inside now. Each holding a place in my history and in my heart.

We set my bags inside the door and head back down to the beauty shop. I'm tired and hot and sticky. I long to go in and take a long, hot shower and then go into my room and stretch out on the bed. Mama's kept it exactly as I left it. But I'm not living by myself anymore and I'll need to get reacquainted with give and take.

She's been chomping at the bit to show me something in the beauty shop. I don't have it in me to ask her to wait until tomorrow.

When we get downstairs, she starts fumbling around in her purse. "You go on in and turn on the lights—you remember where they are, don't you? I think I left my glasses in the car."

She's halfway out the door.

"No, Mama, you set them down on the table just inside the door upstairs. Here, I'll go up and get them—"

She sidesteps me. "I'll get them. You go on in there." And gives me a little push toward the salon door.

Okay. Fine.

The second I open the door, the light switches on, and as if in slow motion, what seems like the entire population of Sago Beach jumps out at me yelling, "Surprise!"

Did I mention how much I hate surprises?

CHAPTER 4

A surprise party.

For me.

As everyone breaks into a rousing chorus of "For She's a Jolly Good Fellow," I cannot begin to explain the utter mortification I feel standing there with every eye in Sago Beach on me. There must be at least fifty people packed in the room—so that's one hundred eyes focused on sticky-and-smelly-from-the-flight me. My hair's uncombed, and I didn't even have a chance to powder the shine off my greasy nose or put on lipstick—

Oh, for God's sake, Mother. Twice in one day?

She sidles up and puts an arm around me as if she senses my discomfort.

After they finish singing, she says in her lyrical voice, "I'll bet the welcoming committee at the airport really threw you off, honey. You weren't expecting this, *huh?*"

Everyone laughs their festive laughs as I stand in the middle of my second surprise party for the day, feeling like I'm stuck in a scene from the movie *Groundhog Day*.

Okay, cool your jets. Just get through this and soon enough you'll be yesterday's news.

"Nope." I plaster a smile on my face. "You really got me, Mama."

Another wave of laughter.

"Tessie, you keep this up, Avril's gonna start expecting a party every day!" Bucky Farley hugs me for the second time today and his hands linger a little too long on my shoulders as he pulls away.

As they crowd around me, a country tune blasts from the sound system. So I may not like surprise parties, but now that the initial sting is over, I sink into the warmth of all these familiar faces. All these kind people here to see...me.

This is what I missed in L.A. This connection to real, salt-of-the-earth folks. People who would drive two hours round-trip to welcome you home after all these years of being away. People who have looked after my mother in my absence. People who will welcome me back into the fold.

All those years in L.A., I never made friends like this, who would love you unconditionally. Sure, I had acquaintances, movie contacts and people I worked with in the various salons, but nothing stuck. Not like this. I always brushed it off to getting older. You know, with wisdom of age comes weariness of heart. You just don't let people in as readily. Right here, right now, it feels good to just be.

I scan the room looking for Kally, but she's not there. Part of me wishes she would've come. That she would've been the one to make the first move toward forgiveness. And how would I have reacted?

"Okay, everyone, let's eat." Mama motions to a table set up in the reception area piled with everything from cheeses, salads and deviled eggs to fried chicken, turkey and roast beef, all the way down to the scrumptious desserts—every kind imaginable, everything homemade. Well, except if you count the Parker House rolls from Paula's Bakery. But considering she made them, they're as good as homemade. "Avril is the guest of honor. Let her go first, and everyone else fall in line after her."

My mother is a feeder. She thinks every problem in the world can be solved with food. If you're happy, she'll feed you. If you're sad, she'll feed you. If you're uncertain about your future, eat and everything will fall into place. So there amidst the cutting stations and the bonnet driers I take my place at the front of the makeshift buffet, feeling like the prodigal daughter returned home.

Once my plate is full, Mama seats me in the place of honor—the center bonnet drier—and assembles a TV tray for my food. If I hadn't fully regressed to preadolescence, with this I have. Completely.

"Mother, I don't want a tray."

She scoots it closer to me. I scoot it back, precariously balancing the paper plate in one hand.

Enough is enough.

I stare her square in the eye to get the message across.

Thank God for Gilda Mathers.

"Tess, stop it. She doesn't want the tray. Take it away or I will."

The two women stare each other down, Gilda with her large frame and short, teased, chestnut hair—à la Kathy Bates. Small, wiry Tess with her long, flaming curls. Never have you seen two women so opposite.

But either one would give her arm for the other. Gilda has been my mother's best friend for as far back as I have cognizant memories; a faithful employee of Tess's Tresses, all-round confidante and second mother to me. She even came out to California a couple of times with Mama to visit me.

Tess's gaze wavers first. She rolls her eyes and shakes her head. Then dutifully folds up the tray and whisks it out of sight. This time Gilda won—thank God in heaven—next time it'll surely be Tess, in that natural give and take of friendship.

Gilda plops into the red Naugahyde dryer seat next to me, with an *umph* and a paper plate piled so high, I'm afraid one wrong move will send everything falling to the floor. Lonnie Sue Tobias and Dani Reynolds, who also work in the beauty shop, pull up folding chairs so that the four of us form a square. They leave the dryer seat to my left free. For Mama.

Dani has the remnant yellow-blue shadows of a fading

bruise around her eye. My heart clenches. She's tried to cover it with concealer, but the discoloration shows through under the florescent lights. It looks like she's had a hard fall or someone's fist connected with her left eye—

"Okay, start talking, missy," says Gilda. "Tell us everything starting with the last time I saw you out there in California. How long's it been now?"

Lonnie Sue scoots forward on her chair. "Must be five years at least. That's when I came down with appendicitis, when you and Tess were off in California. Land, how time flies. Darlin', we're so glad you're home and so is your mama. She can sure use an extra set of hands in the shop. My tinnitus is acting up again and sometimes I take such a spell I can't do nothin' but put a pillow over my head and lay there in the dark with what sounds like the bells of St. Mary's going off in my head."

Gilda frowns around the chicken leg she's biting into. *The Bells of St. Mary's* was a movie. It's not actually a place where they ring bells."

Lonnie Sue wrinkles her pert nose and flicks a strand of cropped eggplant-colored hair off her forehead. "I know that, Gilda, I mentioned it because it *is* a movie. You know, on account of Avril being in the movie business and all."

Oh, no—

"Well, actually, I only worked on a few movies."

Lonnie Sue, Gilda and Dani regard me with confused frowns.

"But you did do Julia Roberts's hair. Right?" demands Gilda.

At the mention of Julia Roberts, the room quiets. Well, it doesn't exactly fall hear-a-pin-drop silent, but those within earshot stop talking and crowd around.

"Well…" I squirm inwardly and wonder what exactly my mother has told them. Because the truth is, I only assisted the stylist who did Julia Roberts's hair on one of the movies she made back in the nineties. I didn't actually have my hands in her hair. And I only got that job because Chet realized how disillusioned I'd become with the whole Hollywood scene and thought if I could get in the middle of *the business*, I'd be happy. He had his work and loved it, so he called in a favor to get me the assistant's job hoping I'd find my place among California's beautiful.

After the Julia Roberts movie, I worked on a few minor projects—the Persephone picture, and a couple others… nothing notable. By then, I'd had it with the industry. If I felt like a fish out of water before Chet dropped me into the great Hollywood shark tank, well, after that I was the fish who *wanted* to dive out of the aquarium. Working in the movies wasn't for me. It was too shallow, too many people willing to take off their clothes and sell their firstborn for a taste of fame. Not at all what a naive, wide-eyed, small-town girl thought it would be. I was pretty much at risk for being eaten alive.

At least by doing hair in salons I was able to build relationships with clients, change someone's outlook by helping them become the best they could be. In the movies, the only reason anyone helped anyone was if it benefited them.

I had nothing in common with these people and it scared me because Chet thrived in this cardboard world. He couldn't understand why I'd *settle for* working at a salon when "if you only tried a little harder, you could make your dream come true."

I didn't always feel this way about California. Chet and I had had big dreams. I was going to be a star and he was going to be my agent. That was our plan—to take Hollywood by storm.

But when the plan didn't work out quite like we thought it would, he took a job at WKGM in the mail room and I tried to land another agent. This is where the irony sets in— I couldn't get work, but they loved him so much that eventually they created the extreme sports segment for him.

For a girl from a small Florida beach town, at first glance Hollywood seemed like Fantasy Land. But it tends to trap people this way. In the beginning, it seduces, whispers sweet nothings—delicious, mouthwatering promises.

I endured one humiliating experience after another—I couldn't crack the reputable agents because of my lack of experience and, okay, I'll admit it was probably because of my lack of raw talent. The only agents who were interested in me were the ones who were out to scam or prostitute me.

It's amazing what some people will do for a taste of perceived stardom. I'm no prude, but I have my standards and it soon became apparent that I did not have what it took to conquer Hollywood. In return, Hollywood had nothing to offer me. There I stood with my nose pressed to the glass of this magnificent candy store, but it was closed, the lids set firmly on the jars, all the goodies stored out of my reach.

For a short time before I came to this sad realization, I thought Chet and I could be happy there.

Chet had became somewhat of a minor celebrity around town and was bitten by the bug. People started recognizing him on the street— "Hey! Aren't you that extreme sports dude on TV? I saw your spot on the ASP Tahiti Surfing Tour. Righteous, dude!"

Fame, minor as it was, was like a drug to him. The more recognition he got, the more he craved. The more remote the location the network sent him to—Fiji, Australia, Hawaii—the more he craved getting away. You know how I feel about flying. So I stayed behind, focusing on how everything would get better once we had a baby.

That was before I knew a baby was out of the question.

"So what's Julia Roberts like?" A voice from the crowd pulls me back, and I realize I don't even know who asked the question.

"Umm…she's very nice. Very down to earth." This is not a lie. I was in close enough proximity that I could ascertain that she's quite pleasant. It's the other people in the industry who weren't so wonderful.

"So will you fix me up with her?" Bucky Farley guffaws.

Someone utters, "Get a life, Farley."

"Well, it doesn't hurt to ask."

"Who else did you work on?" asks Lonnie Sue, all wide-eyed.

"You know, actually, I didn't—"

"Back away, everyone." My mother shoulders her way through the throng with a plate to rival Gilda's. "Let her eat her dinner in peace."

She sits down next to me as if she's settled into her throne. "Avril's home to stay, so you'll have plenty of time to hear all the Hollywood stories. In fact, why don't y'all book an appointment and get your hair done by our very own beauty operator to the stars and hear about it then?

"In the meantime, grab yourselves some of Maybell Jennings's chocolate cake. It's so good on the lips, it's worth carrying it around on the hips."

As the knot of people breaks apart, Lonnie Sue eyes Mama's plate and then bites into a celery stick. "Chocolate cake. Ha. With this thyroid of mine if I even look at cake, I'll pack on five pounds." She pats her belly. "I already have years of Maybell's cakes to contend with."

Mama smiles, then closes her eyes as she savors her first bite of deviled egg.

"Mmmm…what more could a girl want?" She reaches over and pats my leg. "Good food and my darlin' girl. I got everything I need right here."

I glance around the beauty shop, letting its familiarity seep into my bones like a balm. Everything is neat and in its functional place. Mama hasn't redecorated since she opened the place back in seventy-six. But it's clean and painted. Nothing looks too worn or in disrepair.

Someone has yanked down the white sheets I saw hanging when we drove by. As it turns out, they weren't drapes after all, only a temporary prop to curtain off what was brewing inside, so Mama could drive me down Main Street without ruining the surprise. True to form, Tess Mulligan doesn't miss a thing.

"I really never thought I'd see you back here." Dani wrinkles her tanned, freckled nose and looks down at her hands. "I mean, I'm glad you're back, but, well, you know… I guess if I ever got out of here and made it to California I wouldn't want to come back."

I shrug and so does she, nervously flipping her long, straight golden-brown hair over her right shoulder. With that too-long fringe of bangs sweeping across her tanned forehead, she still looks like the natural, pretty beach girl she was when we were in high school. Only a little spent and worn around the edges…

I try to look in her blue eyes rather than at the ring of

bruise, but it's hard to keep my gaze from wandering. Mama never says much about Dani. We weren't very close in school. But I'm surprised she never mentioned Dani coming in with a shiner. I make a mental note to ask her about it. Not simply to gossip, but to see if she needs help.

"Things change," I say.

I glance at her left hand and see she's still wearing a ring. "How's Tommy?"

"Doing good. Still over at the hardware store. He's the manager now."

Dani and Tommy quit high school in the beginning of our senior year after Dani got pregnant. They got married— she had the baby, he took a job at the hardware store.

"Tommy's workin' late tonight. That's the reason he's not here. Had to go on a delivery over to Cocoa. But Renie's here."

Renie?

She motions to a beautiful, willowy blond teenager sitting on the floor on the opposite side of the room. All bad posture and awkward, skinny limbs, she looks like the teen-age version of Dani I remember, only blonder. She's listening to an MP3 player with an expression that suggests this party is the last place she wants to be.

When Dani motions her over, she rolls her eyes and drags herself to her feet, looking downright disgusted by the imposition.

The girl presents herself, but doesn't look up from the iPod she's holding in her right hand.

"Renie, this is Avril," Dani says in her quiet voice. "The party's for her."

I wonder if the girl can hear her mother because the earbuds are still planted firmly in her ears. Dani reaches up and touches her daughter's cheek.

Renie flinches and shoots the look of death at her mother.

"Renie? Remember I was telling you about the girl I used to go to school with who worked in the movies?"

The girl looks me square in the eyes and pulls a *so what* face. "No."

Dani flushes the shade of the Naugahyde.

"Sweetie, why don't you just go on home if you're gonna act like that? I don't want you ruining Avril's party."

Renie turns and walks toward the door.

"You go straight home now," Dani calls after her. "Your daddy should be home soon and I'm going to ask him if you were there when he got home."

Renie doesn't turn around.

Lonnie Sue puts a hand on my arm. "Avril, hon, so you're going to start on Monday?"

I'm glad for the diversion so I won't have to gloss over the awkward Renie moment with Dani.

"I haven't really talked specifics with Mama, but sure, I can start Monday if that's what works."

Gilda stands up stiffly and shoots me a lightning-quick look that suggests she caught the exchange with Renie. Her eyes dart away just as fast, focusing on her paper plate as she folds it in half around the chicken bones like a big white grease-stained taco.

"Actually you're right between the two of us," she says. "So we can both keep an eye on you."

She winks at me. "Well, I don't have a cranky thyroid. So I'm definitely goin' to claim me a piece of Maybell's cake before it's all gone."

As she ambles off, Mama corrals Lonnie Sue and Dani into a discussion about the overbooked schedule on the Saturday of the Founder's Day celebration—which appointments they want to keep and which they want to shift over to me.

I'd wondered how my coming on board would work. The way Mama's been billing me as the "beauty operator to the stars" and urging people to come in and book an appointment with me, I didn't want to step on anyone's toes by poaching their clients. Hairdressers can get a little territorial and the last thing I want to do is get off on the wrong foot.

I'm glad Mama broached the subject and decided to let them figure it out. I get up and circulate, thanking people for coming, talking to others about who married whom, who's divorced and who died—seventeen years worth of gossip to catch up on in one night. Most of it I already know because a leaf couldn't drop from a tree without Mama calling to tell me.

It's wonderful to see everyone, but it's also a little overwhelming. By the end of the party, my head is buzzing. I'm relieved when the last person bids us goodbye, leaving Mama, the girls and me to clean up.

I start gathering used paper plates into a pile.

"What do you think you're doing?" Lonnie Sue stands in front of me with her hands on her hips. "You will not tidy up after your own party. Right, Tess? I'm sure she's exhausted so tell her to get her skinny self upstairs and stretch out on the bed and let us get this place back in order."

All four of them make noises about me leaving them to do the cleanup as they bustle around tidying up in a routine that almost seems choreographed.

"I am tired," I admit. "But I don't think I can sleep just yet. I'd like to take a walk and get a breath of fresh air."

"Oh, honey, it's dark outside," Mama says. "Dani, you go with her. I mean, I'm sure it's safe, but, well…you know how it is." She flutters her long fingers and bends down to retrieve a plastic fork from under one of the chairs.

I'm just opening my mouth to protest, because I really am looking forward to the solitude. What I had in mind was breathing in the fresh night air as I walked down Main Street, reacquainting myself slowly without having to make conversation. But Dani's already got her purse on her arm.

"I'd love to take a walk with you, Avril."

We're mostly silent as we walk the short block up Broad Street toward Main Street.

We turn onto the deserted main drag, pausing in front of the salon's big plateglass windows to watch the three women make quick work of putting the place back in order. They wave at us. We wave back and start walking again.

The street is lit by old-fashioned wrought-iron gas lamps that illuminate the storefronts, allowing just enough light to see inside. We stop again, this time in front of Paula's Bakery.

"Are you going to take back Mulligan?"

It takes a moment to realize she's asking if I'll take back my maiden name. I want to say "I'm a widow, not a divorcée," but instead, I shake my head.

"I want to keep Chet's name. At least it makes me feel like I still have a part of him."

A balmy breeze blows in and I breathe in deeply, savoring the briny ocean scent. I want to ask her about the bruise, but I don't know how.

Instead, we start walking again.

As we turn the corner to complete our circle around the block, the glow of the gas lamps on Main Street doesn't illuminate the small community parking lot that's adjacent to the hardware store. It's dark and a little eerie hearing the crash of the waves off in the distance.

"Oh, good, Tommy's back." Dani gestures to the shadowy

far corner of the lot, and I can just make out the outline of a big, dark pickup. "Renie and I walked to the party since Tommy took the truck. I'll just ride home with him. But, of course, we'll both see you back down the block."

It makes me a bit uneasy thinking that Tommy might have given her that bruise, but it seems worse for her to walk in the dark alone. Of course, one of us could have driven her…

"Let's go around to the back door," she says. "He's probably in the office doing paper work."

She raises her hand to knock, but the door opens and Tommy stumbles out. His long black hair is mussed. His blue button-down shirt is completely open, showing a pelt of dark chest hair that narrows as it disappears beneath the top of his unfastened jeans. Holding a beer bottle in his left hand, he has his right arm draped around the shoulder of a buxom brunette.

CHAPTER 5

Real life never turns out like the movies.

In real life, Superman doesn't swoop down and catch the jumper before she hits the pavement; the governor doesn't call at the last second to grant a stay of execution; and when the husband is discovered rumpled and mussed with a sexy bimbo half his age, you just better accept the fact that the screwing going on in the hardware store had nothing to do with hardware.

Well, not the metallic variety anyway.

Yeah. It pretty much boils down to what you see is what you get, despite all the happy spins the Hollywood scriptwriters have dreamt up. Because let's face it, Sago Beach is about as far removed from Hollywood as you can get. Since there aren't writers lurking behind the sets of our lives to script us off the ledge of emotional suicide, nobody was a bit surprised when Dani called in sick Monday morning.

"Not a problem, hon," Mama said. "Avril will handle your appointments—on a temporary basis. 'Til you feel strong enough to come back to work… Of course we won't say anything to anyone… Right… No, now Dani, whatever's said will come from you. It's not our place to be tellin' your private business…."

Never mind that she'd already told Lonnie Sue and Gilda the entire story, justifying it with, "We're like family here. So y'all need to know what's going on with Dani."

I get the sinking feeling word will spread just like in the old Fabergé organic shampoo commercial from the late seventies where everyone tells two friends and they tell two friends and so on and so on….

Poor Dani. Nothing like having the entire town take a front-row seat while the intimate details of your marital problems unfold center stage.

Mama cradles the phone between her ear and her shoulder and opens the register. As she counts money into the drawer, she nods and says things like, *"Right,"* and *"Um-hm,"* and *"You poor dear."*

I wonder how she can count and listen at the same time.

Gilda, Lonnie Sue and I pretend we're not listening. They're tiding up their stations. I'm setting up all the things I'll need to get started, which is not much—scissors, combs, brushes, blow dryers, flat irons and curling irons. Everything that fit into one suitcase.

I sold my supply of bleach, foil, color and other expendables to the owner of the last salon I worked in, figuring I could restock once I got here.

The bulk of my belongings are on a truck making the cross-country pilgrimage to join me. I sold the car and some of the larger pieces of furniture. I suppose getting rid of the hair dye didn't really lighten the load much, but it seemed the thing to do at the time.

You know, one step closer to making a fresh start. When the furniture gets here, I'll put it in storage. At least for the time being, until I get a place of my own. But for now it feels kind of nice to travel light.

"You don't suppose Dani caught Tommy with that King girl, do you?" asks Lonnie Sue.

Both she and Gilda stop what they're doing and look at me.

The ugly scene of two nights ago replays in my mind and a pang for what Dani must be suffering unfurls inside me. Sometimes I miss Chet so badly it's a physical ache. But seeing how Dani is suffering, I realize at least I still have the sanctity of our marriage to cling to. I don't know which is worse, to loose your love to death or to another woman. Suddenly talking about Dani behind her back doesn't seem right.

As I bend to plug in a curling iron, I say, "I have no idea who *that King girl* is." Instead of looking at them, I check to make sure the button is turned to Off. Then I look through my purse for my lipstick.

"That's Jimmy and Bobbi Nell King's girl. Oh, what was her name…?" In the mirror, I see Gilda's lips tighten into a thin line and I gather there's no love lost there. "I guess you wouldn't know her, seeing how they only lived here a couple or three years. They moved after Mary West caught her husband in a compromising position with *that girl.*"

I think Gilda means to lower her voice, but all she manages to do is duck her head and say in a loud stage whisper, "Seems she has a thing for married men. Was this gal with Tommy a short redhead?"

I shake my head, relieved when Mama hangs up the phone and Gilda and Lonnie Sue turn to her expectantly.

"Well, that was Dani. She's going to take some vacation time." Mama straightens a stack of appointment cards on the desk as she speaks, her eyes averted. Then she plucks a purple feather duster from a drawer and sweeps it around. A nervous gesture that makes me think Mama doesn't want to gossip about it, either.

"Well, who can blame her?" says Lonnie Sue. "After this, let's hope she finally dumps the no good jackass. It's been a long time coming. When she came in here with that black eye, I almost went after him."

Still holding the duster, Mama puts her hands on her hips and shakes her head. "Now look, we need to be respectful of Dani's situation. I'm sure I don't have to ask you to be discreet."

Gilda and Lonnie Sue snort and *tsk*, pulling faces that suggest Mama has cut them to the quick. I put the cap on my lipstick tube, put it back in my purse. Proud of Mama for doing the right thing.

"All rightie then. Avril, I suppose you heard me tell Dani you'd take her appointments today. It'll give you a chance to get acclimated."

She flips the sign on the door to *Open* and unlocks the dead bolt, admitting Maybell Jennings, who's wearing a red headscarf tied beneath her chin.

"Mornin' Ms. Maybell." Gilda motions her client over and pats the chair.

"Well, howdy-do girls." Maybell hefts herself into the chair with an *oomph* and pulls off the scarf, revealing a head full of small gray mesh rollers with pink picks poking out at all angles.

"Just a comb-out today, honey. Hope you got lots of gossip because I'm hungry for it this morning. So dish it up, sweet and juicy."

Gilda shoots Mama a guilty look. Mama raises her brows at her in a don't-you-dare warning that I remember so well from when I was growing up. Gilda gives Mama an almost imperceptible nod of understanding before she starts removing the rollers from the older woman's hair.

Apparently satisfied, Mama walks back to the desk. "Avril, your first client is Marge Shoemaker, but she's not due in for another hour and she's always at least a half-hour late—"

The chime on the door sounds. My stomach lurches

when I see Max Wright, my cowboy airplane seatmate, standing there with his black hat in his hand.

IT'S SUCH A Catch-22, small-town life. At times like this, I realize I have a love-hate relationship with it. I love being part of the fabric in the patchwork quilt that is a community. Still, I hate the way everyone knows your business—sometimes before you do.

Max stands in the doorway, silhouetted by the morning sun. Every gaze in the room is fixed on him. Especially Lonnie Sue, whose face lights up as she locks in on him like a homing device on a target.

Man at eleven o'clock. BeepBeepBeepBeepBeepBeepBeepBeep. Target locked.

"Well, Avril, look who's here to see you," Mama says before Lonnie Sue can launch herself. "It's Max, isn't it?"

All heads swivel from him to me. I stand there like a dolt, not knowing what to say other than, "What are you doing here?"

It sounds wrong. Snippy. I want to explain to him that it's not that I'm unhappy seeing him standing there. In my mother's salon. Knowing he's come all this way. I suppose *surprised* is a better way to put it. I'm surprised. And a little uncomfortable. Embarrassed by the palpable waves of glee radiating off my mother. But before I can utter a word, Gilda says, "I don't suppose you're here for a haircut, are you, darlin'? If so, Avril can take you now. Can't ya, hon?"

A grin tugs at Max's lips. He runs his free hand through his hair. I force myself to hold his gaze.

"Actually, I've come to see if Avril would like to have a cup of coffee with me sometime."

"She's free right now." Lonnie Sue shoves me toward Max. I stumble and whack my hip on the chair at my station.

I don't even have to glance in the mirror to know my face is flushed.

I may have fleetingly forgotten the perils of small-town life, might have been momentarily drawn in by the hunger to be part of that patchwork quilt, but Lonnie Sue's shove jolts me back to reality.

Even though I really don't want to have coffee with Max—or any man who isn't Chet—I'd better get him out of the salon before the girls graduate to the next step which is dragging out my baby photos and old home movies.

"I suppose I'll take a break now."

I brush past him, motioning for him to follow me outside. He does.

Once the door is closed securely behind me, I say, "Well, this is a surprise. What brings you to the 'hood?"

He looks at me for a few beats, and I want to squirm.

"I had to see for myself where Sago Beach's very own beauty operator to the stars holds court."

I shake my head and do my best to suppress a smile.

"Okay then, I understand there's a place nearby that serves the best cup of coffee this side of—" He glances down the street toward the big Founder's Day Celebration banner. "This side of Main Street. Or is that just an urban legend?"

I snort and I'm not even embarrassed.

"Definitely urban legend. Despite the beauty and old-fashioned feel of downtown Sago Beach, there's one thing it lacks."

I arch a brow at him, challenging him to venture a guess.

"A place where you can get a decent cup of joe?"

I nod.

"Uh-oh." He grimaces.

"Oh, wait, it gets worse. Do you know there's not even a place within walking distance where you can get a cup of coffee to go? Totally foreign concept 'round these parts. If you want someone to serve you coffee, you sit down in a booth, drink it out of a sturdy white mug and you don't pay an arm and a leg for it. The folks at the Sago Diner wouldn't dream of asking you to shell out nearly five dollars for a cup of frou-frou that doesn't include all the free refills you care to sit there and drink."

He laughs. "It's a nasty urban legend then."

"Yep, and too bad because if there's one thing the fine people of Sago Beach definitely need, it's a good, strong infusion of caffeine."

His back is to the shop's large picture window, which my mother is now cleaning with a wad of paper towels and a bottle of Windex. She catches my eye.

Suddenly I wish I could take back everything I'd just said.

Who am I to judge?

So snarky.

So superior.

I didn't mean to be so harsh. Even though that wasn't always the case. Before I left seventeen years ago, it seemed to me as if all the locals were walking in their sleep. Sometimes I wanted to give them all a good hard shake and yell, *Wake up! Don't you see that there's so much more to life than this?*

Now, here I am back with the best of them. I didn't exactly set the world ablaze. I guess some might say the laugh's on me.

Mama motions across the street, and mouths *Go!* She points to her watch.

One word comes to mind: *fishbowl.* Again, guilt tugs at me as I weigh the pros and cons of coming home.

"But I suppose good coffee is judged by the buds of the taster," I say.

He nods, puts on his hat. "Well then, why don't we go to the Sago Diner and I'll decide for myself?"

As we wait for a car to pass before we cross the street I ask, "Are you in town on business?"

"Nope, just came over to see you." He jerks a thumb

toward the banner. "To ask you to that Founder's Day dance they're advertising. That is if you don't already have a date."

Oh. This makes me squirm. It makes me feel strange, as if I'm being unfaithful to Chet.

"Well, that's a long way off."

He nods, but doesn't look convinced.

I'm not ready for a man to commute to see me.

I'm not ready to date anyone. Period.

Even if he lives next door.

We cross the street in silence because suddenly I can't think of a thing to say.

I'm glad he doesn't push the dance, but I also have this horror-flash that we're in for a round of bad coffee and stilted conversation because I feel clumsy and tongue-tied.

Harry Philby walks out of the bakery and stops, blatantly eyeing Max up and down. We pass Jillian Lamb and Karen Foster on the sidewalk on the way to the diner. I mumble a quick hello and keep walking because I don't want to be forced to introduce Max.

In the split second as we pass them, I'm sure I see them look at each other, registering: *Avril's taken up with a stranger. Husband's been dead less than a year. How disrespectful to Chet.*

Tanya Adams comes out of the coffee shop as we start to enter. Max holds open the door. Her bulky frame blocks the way, so we have no choice but to stop and talk.

"Well, howdy-do, Avril. Good to see you, sweetie. I'm sorry I couldn't make the party the other night. Hal was home with the creeping crud. Men. They're such babies when they get sick."

She eyes Max as if he's the special of the day at Howard Tilly's butcher shop. "And who might we have here?"

She virtually licks her lips.

I stand there frozen because, for the life of me, I can't remember Max's last name.

"Max Wright." He holds out his hand and smiles.

She grips his fingers and titters, her double chin wobbling like a turkey waddle.

"Did you come home from California with Avril?"

"Yes, I did, as a matter of fact."

I flinch. "Well, not exactly *with* me. I met Mr. Wright on the plane."

This time I cringe.

Mr. *Wright* sounds like Mr. *Right*. Oh, for the love of—

"Well, is that so? How romantic! Some girls wait their entire lives and never meet Mr. Right. You're lucky enough to have had *two* Mr. Rights. You lead a charmed life, ladybug."

"No, that's not what I—"

"Now, don't you worry what anyone might say about it being too soon to jump back into that dating pool. This is not the Victorian age. Chet would've wanted this for you."

"Tanya, Max and I are not—"

"Baby doll, you don't have to explain to me or anyone else. It's none of nobody's business what you two are doing. You're both consenting adults." She jabs a chubby finger at Max. "You just be sure you treat her right if you know what's good for you. She's been through too much heartbreak already. There's a lot of people around here who'll skin you alive if you hurt our Avril."

He crosses his arms and flashes a smile.

"Oh, my intentions are perfectly honorable. Don't you worry about that."

I'm absolutely immobilized by the scene unfolding in front of me. Immobilized and horrified. I want to say something. I know I *should* say something.

For that matter, why doesn't *Mr. Right-Wright* set her straight instead of egging her on?

"Oh, would you look at the time," says Tanya. "I have to run." She cocks her head to the side and flashes a coy grin. "*Mr. Right.* Oh, it's so romantic. You kids restore my faith in love. Toodles."

She sighs as she brushes by us.

Max runs a hand over his face, but I can still see his grin.

"You think it's funny?" I ask.

He shrugs. "The way I see it, if you don't laugh, you'll scream. Trust me. It always works out better when you laugh."

He holds open the door and sweeps a hand forward.

"Welcome to Sago Beach," I mutter under my breath.

Max chooses a booth at the front of the restaurant. I start to suggest moving to one along the back wall where we won't be so conspicuous, but decide against it because it might look a little too cozy. Then I waver again, mad at myself for caring how other people might misconstrue my having coffee with him when it's none of their business.

But Max is already settled, so I slide into the booth, too.

There's a handful of customers in the diner. I'm relieved when none of them pay much attention to us.

My heart clenches as Carrie Fields starts toward us with two menus. I went to high school with her. She's one of the few people I graduated with who stayed in Sago Beach. Most people my age had the good sense to get out: those who wanted a life, anyway.

Inwardly, I squirm for a few seconds, wishing for a way out, but finally realize there's no escaping her inevitable inquisition.

"Well, if it isn't Avril Carson." She smiles. "It was a fun party the other night. I know your mama's real happy you're back."

"Hi, Carrie."

She slants an eager glance at Max, who's reading the menu, then quirks a brow at me, her expression a question mark.

"Just coffee for me."

She pulls an oh-come-on-who's-your-friend face. When I don't introduce Max she turns to him and says, "And for you Mr....?"

Great, here we go again.

Max closes the menu. "Max Wright. I take it you didn't catch the conversation with Tanya?"

I kick him under the table, but that doesn't knock the smile off his face.

"Nope, I guess I missed that one." Her inflection turns up at the end of the sentence, providing a do-tell-I'm-all-ears invitation. And I'm sure she'll stand here all day to get the scoop if he'll dish.

Thank God he says, "Just coffee for me, too, please."

She sighs and ambles off shaking her head.

The diner smells of bacon, toast and coffee with a base note of stale cigarette smoke still lingering from the days when they allowed people to smoke in here.

"Ah, the beauty of small-town life." He nods in Carrie's direction. "We should've invited her to join us."

I raise my brows. "You're a troublemaker, aren't you?"

His eyes twinkle. "Who, me? Of course not."

I study him for a moment, trying to size him up. He's a lot cuter than I remember. I wonder if he's the kind of guy who always has to be the center of attention? I pull a napkin from the silver holder and brush some stray salt granules off the table.

"So, who's the *other* Mr. Right Tanya was talking about?"

Chet.

The thought of him pierces me.

I stare at the napkin in my hand and do my best to stave

off the wave of sadness. One of the things I haven't been able to get used to since my husband died is how grief blind-sides me. I'll be minding my own business, thinking I'm fine, then all of a sudden—*wham!* Grief sneaks up from behind and slams me to the mat.

I start twisting the napkin into a tight spiral, needing something to do with my hands.

"It's a long story I really don't want to get into right now."

Max nods.

The overhead florescent lights buzz, bright and unforgiv-ing, making me feel exposed—like a cheat for sitting here with this man I barely know.

But how can I be a cheat when my husband is dead?

Carrie brings the coffeepot and two white mugs, which she sets down with a careless clatter, then *thunks* down the silver cream pitcher. Some coffee sloshes over the rim of the cups as she pours.

"Anything else?"

"No, Carrie. Thank you."

She casts another curious glance at Max, who winks and sends her tittering all the way back to the kitchen.

"You just made her day."

Max chuckles. "You know what I find most curious about small towns?"

I toss the wadded napkin to the side and put my hands in my lap, waiting for my coffee to cool. "What?"

"When you come back after being gone for a while, it seems like everyone's second-guessing your every move, staring at you like you're an alien or some exotic animal that's escaped from the circus. But I don't really mind. It's good to be home and that's just part of the charm."

I pick up my cup and blow into the muddy liquid.

"So where is this circus you escaped from?" I ask.

"Los Angeles."

I shake my head. "You don't seem very L.A."

"I'm not. I was born and raised in Kissimmee, Florida, which is not such a small town anymore—but not so unlike Sago Beach. Have you heard of Kissimmee? It's famous for a number of fine things."

"Such as?"

He looks surprised. "Rodeos and cows. It's better known as Cow-simmee. It has the heart of a small town. But, no matter how big it gets, it will always be a big little cow town. Where everyone knows everyone."

"Kind of like here," I say. "But with cows."

He nods and blows on his coffee.

"I gather you're not very fond of it?" I ask.

He shakes his head. "On the contrary. When I left for L.A., I would've told you different. I couldn't get away fast enough."

"I know how it feels." I nod, but then in the blink of an eye, I decide I don't want to know more about why he left.

I don't want to get that personal. "So is it any easier now that you're back?"

"Yeah, I think it is. It doesn't bother me as much now. In fact, knowing my neighbors is a welcome change from L.A."

We both look out the diner window as Helen Caferty walks by. She waves at us, turning her head to register the stranger.

"Isn't it funny how everyone waves in a small town?" he says. "It's kind of universal. They don't even have a clue who you are, but they wave anyway."

I give a half shrug, staring out the window. "That's just their way of saying, 'I see you, stranger. I'm keeping an eye on you.'"

Out the window, I watch Joe Roberts set out goods in front of the hardware store, his horn-rims sliding down the bridge of his nose. He pushes the glasses up with one hand and waves to a passing car with the other. It's Emma Pope rolling by at a snail's pace, hands gripping the wheel at ten and two. She gives him the raised index finger salute. The scene makes me smile.

"See, everybody waves," Max says. "I know the routine. I grew up with it." His brown eyes twinkled. "If you're not careful, you catch yourself waving at the cows."

"Thank God we don't have cows in Sago Beach."

"Lucky you. Because when the cows start waving back, that's when you know it's time to leave."

The conversation wanes. I almost ask why he left Kissimmee. But I don't. There are a lot of things I could ask him—

that I *should* ask—all in the spirit of polite conversation. What did he do in L.A? Why did he come back? But something—perhaps it's Persephone reaching up from the depths of hell—nudges me and whispers, *You've already asked him enough questions. Don't go there. Not even in the name of polite conversation.*

Still, I hear myself asking, "So are you back in Kissimmee to stay?"

He shifts, stretching one arm along the back of the booth.

"I'm here for the time being. Until you let me take you to that dance…or at least out to dinner."

Since I refused to listen to her before, this time Persephone reaches out and grabs what's left of my threadbare heart and absconds with it into the bowels of hell, leaving me cold and empty and shaky, void of any desire except the overwhelming need to flee.

"I'm sorry," I say. "I have to go. My client's waiting for me."

CHAPTER 6

"If a good-looking guy like that asked me out for coffee, I certainly wouldn't have run away like a scared rabbit." Lonnie Sue looks at me while she back-combs her eleven o'clock's hair into a great, gray monolith.

"I didn't run like a scared rabbit." I fist my hands into the frothy hair I'm shampooing, taking care not to pull it or dig my fingernails into the woman's scalp. The second of Dani's appointments I've taken today, this one drove in from Cocoa Beach. I don't even know her. So she certainly doesn't deserve to get her hair pulled because I'm getting a flogging for my reluctance to jump back into the dating pool.

"You may have walked across that street, darlin'," Lonnie Sue says, "but deep down inside, that scared little bunny wanted to hightail it as fast as she could. I mean, why else would you have lied to Max, saying you had an appointment waiting when you didn't?"

I shrink under the heat of the skeptical gazes waiting for an answer—Mama, Lonnie Sue, Gilda and their three clients. Oh, and let's not forget Ms. *Do-Tell* eagerly gazing up at me from the shampoo bowl.

"I am not having this conversation right now." I turn on the water and watch the lather dissipate and circle the drain.

Okay, so maybe I was a *little* unnerved. Maybe that's why I resorted to the *teensy* white lie about the waiting appointment.

A lot of good it did.

Max saw right through it. "I thought your next client wasn't due for an hour? We haven't even been here twenty minutes."

By that time, I was already out of the booth, edging toward the door with a quick, "Thanks for the coffee."

The fake client excuse was better than running away… *like a scared rabbit.*

Oh, just leave me alone.

"You know, Avril—" Gilda stands there with one hand cocked on her hip, pointing her scissors at me "—You should be flattered that man would drive all this way just to have coffee with you."

I wrap a towel around my client's wet head and help her sit up. "Whose side are you on?"

Gilda smiles and draws up a section of hair with the comb, ready to cut it. "I'm on the side of love. Is there any other place to be?"

Inside me Persephone chastises, *She's right. It shouldn't freak you out.*

I frown. *Okay, enough out of you. If you're on their side,*

*you are not welcome in my thoughts. So help me, I'll find a way
·to drown you out. Because all this talk about men and dating
makes me so darned uncomfortable I wish I could sprout wings
and fly away.*

And you know how I hate to fly.

As I walk my client over to the chair, I take a deep breath
to ground myself, trying to draw reassurance from the
comforts of home—that even though Chet is gone, some
things remain constant.

Tess's Tresses is still the same after all these years. It still
smells the same: a mélange of burnt coffee, Aqua Net hair-
spray and the vague traces of permanent wave solution;
Mama still plays country music on the boom box behind the
reception desk; she still serves the same Danish shortbread
cookies, the kind in the blue tin—there they are sitting
open next to the automatic-drip coffeepot, powdered non-
dairy creamer and various packets of sugar and sweeteners.
I walk over to get my client a cup of coffee and grab a piece
of shortbread from the crimped white-paper cookie cups
peeking over the edge of the blue tin, like a lacy slip
showing—only upside down.

I bite into the cookie and consider the irony—maybe
it's an omen. Now that Chet is gone, will everything feel
upside down?

"So, Miss *I'm Not a Scared Rabbit*, when *are* you going to
see him again?" Lonnie Sue asks.

I shake my head.

"What does that mean?" Mama pauses, holding the curling iron like a scepter.

"Let me make myself clear: *Never*."

All six women in the salon spear me with incredulous stares.

"Well, if you don't want him, I do," Lonnie Sue says. She's in her mid-forties, but just as boy-crazy as the first day her hormones kicked in.

"Fine with me. You can have him."

The salon door bangs open with such force the glass reverberates and the door chimes echo like the discordant bells of hell.

Dani stands just inside the threshold looking like a crazed woman in dirty sweatpants and a stained T-shirt.

She must have had one rough night.

Her brown hair looks greasy and matted, sticking up in places. She looks as if she hasn't slept in a while and traces of smudged mascara give her a ghoulish edge.

"Who told Maybell Jennings about me and Tommy?" She slurs the words.

We stand there gaping at her and glancing at each other like squirrels caught in the middle of the road, unsure of which way to run.

"Tess, you promised!" Dani screams the words with such ferocity I almost expect her head to start spinning. "And now the entire town knows."

Mama rushes over and tries to comfort her. "Honey, I didn't tell a soul—"

Dani pushes Mama away and staggers backward in the process. "Well, somebody did because Maybell Jennings came over with a Bundt cake from the bakery, spoutin' off about how me catching Tommy cheating was a blessing in disguise and how I'd be better off without the no-good son of a bitch." She draws in a ragged breath. "How could you do this to me?"

"Honey, I told you, I didn't. Here, why don't you and me go in the back room, and I'll get us some coffee."

Mama gives Gilda an *I'll deal-with-y'all-later* look as she tries to shepherd Dani into the back room.

"I didn't do it." Gilda holds up both hands. "I swear, I didn't breathe a word to Maybell."

Mama doesn't see Dani's flying fist until it connects with her right cheekbone. She falls and smacks her head on the corner of the desk as she goes down. It all happens so fast and the next thing we know, Dani is on her, swinging and cussing.

In a storm of shouts and clicking heels, Gilda, Lonnie Sue and some of the clients are helping me pull Dani off my mother. The stench of alcohol, perspiration and Dani's unwashed hair burns my nose. A flailing arm connects with my jaw. I see stars for a few seconds.

"You just settle down there," Gilda yells, yanking Dani's arm back so hard, I'm surprised she doesn't dislocate Dani's shoulder. "You have no right to come in here acting like this. Hitting Tess, making such a ruckus. Any more of that and I'll call the sheriff."

Gilda's reprimand distracts Dani long enough for Lonnie Sue and me to get a firm grip on her. Once we have her under control, the clients leave Dani to us and go over to check on Mama, who is bent over holding her eye.

"Dani, you should be ashamed of yourself," Gilda mutters as she assesses Mama's injuries.

That sets off Dani again. "Y'all bunch a gossiping bitches. I should mess up your lives like you've messed up mine. Tellin' the whole town my business."

She struggles, but doesn't break free from the hold Lonnie Sue and I have on her.

Thank God.

She looks out of her mind, like a wild animal that would kill whoever was in her path.

"She's drunk." Gilda shakes her head, grabs the phone and dials. "Jean, we have a situation over here at Tess's. Can you send the sheriff as quick as possible...? It's Dani Reynolds—she's pretty well sauced, beating on Tess and talkin' crazy...."

Suddenly, Dani goes limp, dissolving into a heap of sobs.

"Sure, I'll hold." Gilda cups Mama's chin in her hand and looks at the shiner that's already forming. "She's calling Sid on the radio right now." She nods to her client. "Go get some ice for Tess's eye, will ya?"

Mama looks stunned. Wiggling out of Gilda's grasp, she blinks and gingerly touches her eye.

"Yes, Jean, I'm here…." Gilda says. "Okay, thanks…. Well, it's a long story that I don't care to repeat, seeing how that's what set off Dani in the first place. Just tell Sid to hurry, okay?"

"Y'all just couldn't keep your big, fat mouths shut, could ya?" Dani mutters through the sobs. She makes a halfhearted attempt to pull free, but Lonnie Sue and I hang on and she gives up, slumping to the floor. "Y'all just *haaad* to talk, didn't ya? Just *haaad* to tell everyone… I kept my mouth shut about Kally and Chet. But y'all just *haaad* to go blabbin' my business…."

"Dani!" Mama yells. "Hush up. You're drunk and you don't know what you're saying."

Whoa, what about Kally and Chet?

I know I shouldn't pay any attention to what she's saying because she *is* drunk and she's mad and hurting, but it's the look on Mama's and Gilda's and Lonnie Sue's faces that makes me ask, "Dani, *what* about Chet and Kally?"

Dani throws her head back and makes a gurgling, guttural sound somewhere between a laugh and a howl. "Oh, my God! You stupid, stupid bitch. How can you pretend you don't know? We wives…we always know…."

She makes that laugh-howl sound again, but it dissolves into sobs. All of a sudden, Gilda, Mama and Lonnie Sue are all over her. Their words are flying so fast I don't know who's saying what.

"Shut up, Dani."

"You're drunk, Dani."

"Don't do this, Dani. You know there's no proof."

Proof? Oh, my G— All the blood drains from my face, and the room starts spinning.

"At least Tommy's slut wasn't my very own best friend," Dani slurs.

"What?" A crazed panic washes over me. I look from my mother to Gilda to Lonnie Sue and back to my mother. "What is she talking about? Tell me!"

"Stupid, stupid bitch." Dani laughs.

"Get her out of here," Mama yells.

"No!" I insist. "I want to know what she's talking about."

Still, Lonnie Sue and Gilda try to pull a limp Dani to her feet, but I hold on to her, making it impossible.

"You really want to know?" Dani looks at me through slitted eyelids.

Gilda presses her hand over Dani's mouth.

"Shut up, girl! You're drunk. Avril, she's drunk, don't listen to her."

My whole body is shaking. "If it's nothing, then let her talk."

Gilda shakes her head and I see her press her hand tighter to Dani's mouth. Then the next thing I know Gilda screams and yanks her hand away.

"She bit me!"

"Oh, good God, she broke the skin," Lonnie Sue wails.

The clients are cowering in the corner as if they fear for their own lives.

Lonnie Sue lets loose of Dani to help Gilda, who looks as if she's about to faint. All of this is happening around me, but I'm so numb I can't move.

"What about Chet and Kally?" I manage to choke out.

Dani sits there slumped over, swaying a little, but she seems to have lost the anger that was propelling her to fight.

"Kally's kid?" Her voice is a lost whisper. "Well, your golden-boy husband, Chet, he's the daddy of Kally's baby. But I'm not blabbin' because everyone in town already knew that dirty little secret. They just weren't telling you."

My whole body goes numb and the edges of my vision turn a hazy gray.

"How's that make *you* feel, Ms. Beauty Operator to the Stars?"

CHAPTER 7

Years ago, when I had a problem or I needed time to think, I walked on the beach. Something about that vast ocean made my problems seem small.

Maybe they *were* small and inconsequential. Because today as I try to walk some sense into the damning shocker Dani just spilled, even the great Atlantic doesn't seem capable of washing away the layers of hurt.

The beach is deserted, except for a flock of squawking gulls. It sounds like they're gossiping about Dani's revelation as they run in and out of the briny tide.

It's overcast, which makes the sky, sand and water look gray.

Everything is gray.

The light has been stolen.

As a cool wind whips in from the ocean, I get the overwhelming feeling my life will never have color again. Like the reverse of colorizing movies. See—there's that "upside down" theory again.

See? What did I tell you?

It's as if all the hues have been removed from life until

nothing but black and white remains—and all those damn shades of gray in between.

Kally and Chet?

A baby?

Well, he's not a baby anymore. He has to be, what, four years old now?

I kick off my black Prada thong sandals—the ones that once upon a time seemed like such a find at that Hollywood consignment shop over on Ventura Boulevard.

They fly through the air and I leave them where they land. Someone else can have them. I don't want them anymore.

I don't want anything that reminds me of him. Of then. Of what used to be. Because as far as I'm concerned, it's gone. It's all gone.

First, I lost my husband.

Now I've lost what was left of my foundation. I feel it crumbling around me like the sand shifting under my feet. Still, I can't decide what's the worst part:

A) Learning my husband cheated.

B) Knowing my one-time best friend slept with my husband and had his child.

C) Or finding out that my mother has known about this all along and kept it a secret for four or five years.

"Avril, honey, woo-hoo!" I turn around and see my mother waving her arms over her head as she trots toward me. Her eye is so bad I can see from a distance that it's bruised and swollen shut.

The sight of her coming after me sets off a ridiculous pang that tries to guilt me out of being mad at her.

But I *am* mad. So mad I can't talk right now. She betrayed me. I will not feel sorry for her. Even if she does look like she got the tar beaten out of her.

I tear up, but it's just because the wind is whipping my hair into my eyes. I swipe at the moisture with an angry hand. *Damn wind.* Turning away from my mother, who is now only about twenty feet away from me, I walk toward the water.

"Avril, honey, please talk to me."

She's following me.

"Go away." The wind snatches my voice and carries it away so even my anger loses its heat and color.

"We have to talk about this."

At the water's edge, the sea foam laps over my feet, wicking up the legs of my jeans. But I don't care.

"I can't talk to you right now."

Her hand is on my shoulder, fisting into my shirt, and I know if I turn around and see her broken face I'll cave in.

"Please, baby, let me explain."

She lied to me. One of the two people in this world I trusted unconditionally lied to me.

"Go away!" I yank out of her grasp and walk right into the cold water, clothes and all.

"Avril, what are you doing?" She sounds panicked. "Come out of the water."

"Go away, Mama."

I wade out until the water is up to my waist and the wind mutes her protests, but the urgent intonation of her voice carries—even if I can't distinguish the words—like the squawk of the gulls circling above.

I duck under so I don't have to listen to any of it.

Underwater, I hear nothing but the whooshing tide. My clothes feel heavy, weighted down. I open my eyes against the stinging salt, making myself endure the pain, which is nothing compared to the anguish of watching what was left of my world come crashing down around me. So instead, I stay under, watching my hair float like strings of seaweed, drawing my knees to my chest into fetal position, like the baby Chet and I were never able to conceive. Like the baby he had with Kally.

I stay that way until my lungs burn for air. Maybe if I hold my breath just a little bit longer all the pain will disappear.

Wait a minute. That's crazy. If I become fish food, I won't get the chance to confront Kally.

I want to see her face when she realizes I know what she did.

I break the surface, gasping, drinking in greedy gulps of air and shivering. Squeezing my eyes against the sting of the salt, I push my hair out of my face, then blink toward the shore.

Mama's not there anymore.

Good.

I've got time to think.

A small swell rises around me. I fall back into its gentle lift, floating in the ocean, staring up at the gray, sunless sky. The water in my ears closes out the world.

My mind is so full, all my thoughts lodged so tightly in my head, that I can't extract a single one. So I float mindlessly for who knows how long, weightless, watching the gulls fly across that flat, gray canvas of sky. I'm all alone the world. Just me with the big hole left where my heart used to—

Splash. Splash. Splash.

"What the hell—?"

Suddenly something or someone grabs me around the waist, pulling me under for an instant before I realize it's a person—a man—hauling me on his back like a sack of very wet flour or sand or—

"Hey!" I try to protest, but end up drinking in a mouthful of seawater and choking. My God, I couldn't bring myself to end it all earlier, but this guy might just drown me.

Funny the absurd things that run through your mind when the world is a blur of water and coughs. For a chilling second, I wonder if Dani has come out to kill me. But judging by the wide, khaki-clad back, it's not Dani. And she was in no shape to hire a hit man when the sheriff hauled her off.

The next thing I know, I'm lying flat on my back on the

sandy shore. Sheriff Sid Olsen is standing over me panting like a wet dog. The faces of my mother, Gilda, Lonnie Sue and Betty Hagar, complete with foils in her hair and a purple salon cape, crowd into view above me.

I sit up as fast as I can, afraid the sheriff might try to give me mouth-to-mouth. As I shove my wet, sandy hair out of my face, through salty, stinging eyes I see there are more people than I first realized standing around gaping at me.

I can clearly envision my mother running into the beauty shop and telling the sheriff I was drowning.

Oh, for the love of—

Mama launches herself at me. Sobs wrack her body as she holds me.

"Oh, my God, you scared me. I can't believe I almost lost you."

A tinge of guilt tries to worm its way into my anger. *But she lied to me.*

I push out of her embrace and into a standing position, nearly losing my footing in the wet sand. My clothes are waterlogged and heavy.

"I was not drowning. I was…floating. Mama, I can't believe this. I'm so embarrassed."

She's still crying and her eye looks even worse than it did when she first followed me out here.

"I thought you were trying to…" Her good eye is traced with redness, she bows her head and bawls into her hands.

"Oh, for God's sake," I say. "Don't be ridiculous."

Gilda puts an arm around her and Mama buries her face in Gilda's shoulder. Gilda shoots me a lethal glare.

"She thought you were trying to kill yourself. On account of the news about Chet."

"I was not—"

Oh, great. Fresh gossip. Did you hear Avril found out about Chet and Kally's affair and tried to kill herself?

Oh, yeah, that's rich.

How quickly I forget. I'm back in Sago Beach—the place where every action is scrutinized, recorded and filed away so the dossier can be pulled out at a whim and frowned upon and gossiped about in hushed *can-you-believe-that* whispers.

"What kind of a stupid stunt was that?" Gilda demands. "Traipsing off into the ocean fully dressed? Staying underwater like that? What was your mama supposed to think?"

I stand there shamefaced for a moment. Then claustrophobia sets in. I back up a few steps.

"*Dammit,* I was just trying to get away so I could think—" My voice breaks as thoughts of what drove me to the beach crash down like angry waves. "For God's sake, can't I have a moment's privacy?"

Everyone, including Mama, stares at me like I'm a lunatic.

For the second time today, the overwhelming urge to run strangles me. I meet my mother's gaze. Hold it. I want to ask her how she could keep a secret like that from me all these years. She knew. She knew that the entire town knew and still she didn't tell me?

"Okay, folks, show's over," says Sid. "Let's clear out. Give Avril some privacy."

I back up a few more steps.

"No. No, that's okay," I say. "I'll go."

I turn around and start walking. I have no idea where I'm going. I have no car. No place to go. I'm simply walking.

CHAPTER 8

The moment I step through the purple-and-chartreuse-painted front door of Lady Marmalade's Coffeehouse, the head of steam I'd built up on the long march from Sago to Cocoa Beach evaporates.

I guess I wasn't expecting such a crowd this late in the afternoon. Actually, I don't know what I expected. But the place smells of rich, overpriced coffee and buzzes with people—It sounds like the hissing espresso machine is asking, "Why are you here?" I grow a little claustrophobic as I count fourteen people placing orders or sitting at tables, sipping coffee, talking or reading. They've all come for a late-afternoon dose of exorbitant caffeine brewed by the adulterous bitch who's shattered what's left of my life.

Speaking of Kally—I glance around the place looking for her. There's a tall, young surfer-type and a thin, earthy-looking young woman working behind the bar. But I don't see her. *Dammit.* Maybe she's not here....

I move to the side to let customer number fifteen enter and I step in something warm and sticky.

"Uggh!"

My gaze drops to my sand-caked bare feet. I grab a hold of a nearby table for balance and rake my foot like a bull ready to charge, trying to wipe off the repulsive goo. Sand powders the floor and the woman sitting at the table gives me a dirty look.

I point at her. "*You* don't even know the half of it."

She grabs her coffee and moves to a different table.

The espresso machine hisses again. This time it's really mad. *Look at yourself. You're disgusting. Didn't you see the sign outside? No shoes, no service. Go home and put on those Prada sandals that made you feel so superior. Oops! You left them on the beach. Well, then go home and take a shower.*

Yep. I am a mess. A great big emotional and physical wreck. That's why I can't go home—even if I had a home to go to. I must do what I came to do, because if I wait a minute longer to confront Kally Fuller, I'm likely to do damage to myself or my mother or anyone else who tries to justify how in hell they could keep this dirty little secret from me.

I see *her* before she sees me.

She steps out of a side room connected to the bar, carrying a large bag of coffee beans. I almost don't recognize her and probably wouldn't have if not for the blue eyes.

She looks thin and tired, with dark circles under her eyes. Growing up, she was always a little on the chunky side. Not fat, just meaty and big-boned. Now it looks like there's not a spare ounce of beef on those bones. But it's her hair that throws me. It's short—I mean crew-cut short. As she dumps the bag of coffee beans, I see a series of bruises on her forearms. At first glance they almost look like tattoos. God, what's wrong with her?

My first thought is *drugs*. Heroin? She looks *that* bad. But she's definitely lucid, smiling and laughing with customers—regulars, from the looks of it. I guess timid little Kally Fuller has finally come in to her own. Finally lost the baby fat and adopted a funky style to go with her funky little coffee house.

Man-grubbing bitch.

She takes a guy's order, flirts with him as she pours his coffee. She's in her element, happy and carefree, making conversation and spending quick comebacks like small change.

The dam containing my anger breaks and the rage gushes out like floodwaters.

That's when she sees me.

At first, it's a welcoming glance.

Come in! Come in! What can I serve you?

But when she realizes it's me, she freezes; what little color she had drains from her face. And I know instantly the answer to the question I've come to ask.

She seems to move in slow motion as she unties her apron and hangs it on a hook behind the bar.

Traitor.

Adulterous bitch.

Husband-poaching whore.

Do you not have any morals? Any regard for the friendship we used to share?

If this were a movie, I'd scream this at her and everyone in the place would know what she's done, that she's capable of lying and stealing and ruining lives.

But this isn't a film and the words wedge in the back of my throat. All I can do is stand there, swiping at the big, ugly tears that roll down my cheeks.

She whispers something to Surfer Boy. He glances at me warily, as if he's trying to decide whether he should do something about me.

Kally stops to speak to a customer, putting on a fake happy face as if she's innocent.

I have to look away. My gaze lights on the menu—a big gilt-framed blackboard with drink offerings written in colored chalk:

LADY MARMALADE—*cappuccino*

MOCHA CHOCOLATA—*café mocha*

SOUL SISTER—*café latte*

FLOW SISTER—*frappé*

BLACK SATIN SHEETS—*coffee of the day*

CAFÉ AU LAIT—*coffee with milk*

SAVAGE BEAST—*espresso shot*

GREY FLANNEL—*chai latte*

GIVE IT A GO JOE—*Café Americano*
                    (*espresso with hot water*)

GITCHIE GITCHIE YA YA—*caramel latte*

MAGNOLIA WINE—*house wine*

DIAMOND WINE—*premium wine*

Oh, my God, I get it. All the menu offerings are taken from the song "Lady Marmalade." You know, the tune about the prostitute. This is positively surreal.

"The money's an investment in her business. We're all the family she has now, Avril. She needs our help."

"Chet, no. I'd love to help her, but we're barely making ends meet as it is. As much as I love Kally, we can't afford it."

He went behind my back and sent the damn whore money anyway.

And Kally's still talking.

A fresh spiral of ice-cold anger twists through my veins. But despite everything, I realize I really don't want a public scene. That's why I didn't just storm the place like a buccaneer in an old pirate movie.

Still, with each second that she stands there nonchalantly talking, my patience runs thinner. Until I decide she has exactly one minute before I march over there and make her walk the plank in front of her customers.

One minute, starting now—

I look at my wrist and realize I'm not wearing my watch. So I look around the room as I count— One Mississippi, two Mississippi, three Mississippi…

I take in Chet's private investment. The walls are washed a bright red, faux finished, and resemble a New Orleans brothel. I suppose she's keeping with the Lady Marmalade theme.

Fifteen Mississippi, sixteen Mississippi, seventeen Mississippi…

Shabby chic tables, plush reading chairs in ruby, amethyst, sapphire and emerald stand proud, and the Picasso-esque paintings in ornate gilt frames hang on the wall above tags the size of business cards. I move closer to examine one.

Title: The Betrayal.

I wince at the irony, whirling away from the ugly painting.

Okay, her minute's up. I've waited long enough.

I start to walk over to her, just as the customer she was talking to takes her coffee and biscotti to a table.

As Kally rounds the bar, the fake smile is gone, exchanged for the tight, drawn expression. Her cheeks are hollow. My God, she's so skinny. She still walks with a limp, from the time she wrecked her mom's car when we were coming home from Rusty's Bait and Raw Bar, a dive where we used to hang out occasionally. How long has it been since the last time I saw her? A good fifteen years? At least. Back when they used to tease us and say, "Hey look, it's the blonde leading the blonde." Back when I was young and naive, before it dawned on me how offensive that statement really was.

Why did she do that to her hair? It used to be so beautiful. That perfect shade of sun-kissed honey with natural paler highlights. A color only nature can bestow. I know, because I've tried in vain to replicate the shade on my dirty blond hair and hundreds of customers—to no avail.

Each move she makes is like a stop-motion sequence, frozen frame-by-frame—her unwavering stare; the firm set of her jaw; the aura of defiance in her posture, almost as if to spite the limp that always made her so painfully self-conscious.

Scenes from the night we had the wreck flash in my mind. She spent two weeks in the hospital. All I got was a few bumps and bruises.

Kally was always the pretty one—even if she didn't know it. But I had the confidence she lacked. For practical purposes, confidence trumped looks every time.

Where's my confidence now?

I run a hand through my hair, thick and sticky from the dried saltwater. My clothes are stiff-dry, compliments of walking against the briny wind. My jeans stick to my inner thighs and have rubbed me raw. As she stands in front of me, I realize I must look like the Creature from the Black Lagoon materialized from the bowels of the ocean, barefoot and crusty with sand and salt.

"Avril."

I open my mouth to speak—*Deny the hateful rumors that my dead husband is the father of your child.*

The words fade like old celluloid until there is nothing left of them.

She knows why I'm here. I can see it in her eyes, this woman who was my friend, who was like my sister—sisters from different mothers, we used to say... Soul Sisters. Put that on your menu, Lady Marmalade.

I finally manage to choke out, "The boy. Is he the reason Chet was sending you money?"

Kally narrows her eyes as if this is a trick question.

"Answer me." My voice raises a few decibels. "Was my husband sending you child support, when he was pretending to invest in your business?"

People are looking at us.

Kally's eyes dart around the room. The fake smile graces her lips again. She murmurs, "Let's go in my office."

I shake my head. "Answer my question, Kally." The espresso machine screams and hisses. "Did you sleep with my husband?" Then I realize it's not the machine making that terrible noise, but my own keening, which Kally answers by turning around and limping toward a door along the back wall.

A violent, wounded beast rears up inside me, wanting to attack her, but she's too far away. "Answer me, Kally!"

She doesn't even turn around before she disappears inside the office, leaving the door open and my anger impotent.

Surfer Boy steps in front of me. "Hey, be cool, okay? We don't need people yelling. Maybe you should go."

I grit my teeth. "I'm not going anywhere until she tells me whether she slept with my husband."

I try to sidestep him, but he grabs my wrist.

"Let go of me!"

He tightens his grip and my hand goes numb under the force. A couple of customers stand at the ready to help him throw me out.

"Maybe you didn't hear me," Surfer Boy says. "It's time for you to go—"

"Let go of her, Zane." In the commotion, I didn't realize Kally had come out of the office. But there she stands, wringing her bony hands.

Brazen whore.

Her voice is calm, the two red patches on her cheeks belie her composure. She always flushed when she got nervous.

"Avril, we can talk, but you'll have to come into my office." She looks me square in the eyes. "You're not going to make a scene in my coffeehouse."

A challenge: *I mean it.*

She nudges Zane, and he lets go of me. Reluctantly. Eyeing me with distaste and warning: *I'm watching you.*

"It's okay, everyone." There's that fake smile again. My

hand flexes, wanting to slap it off her face. "I'm sorry for the disturbance. Just a misunderstanding."

You are such a liar.

She turns back to me, only this time, she looks past me, somewhere over my shoulder. "Shall we take this into my office, Avril?" Her voice is low, barely above a whisper. "Or shall Zane show you the door?"

Like hell he will.

I open my mouth to tell her we'll have this out right here, right now. On my terms.

But Surfer Boy hulks at the ready, poised to drag me outside if I stray beyond the two options she's so neatly presented. And the room is silent as a church; Kally's faithful disciples stare at me, the crazed lunatic who threatens the beloved Queen of Coffee.

My throat tightens, and I don't trust my voice.

Mute and defeated, I follow her to the back of the café, knowing the writing is on the wall as plain as the faux Picassos. I know what she's going to say. Still, I need to hear her say it. I need to see her eyes when she does.

I don't care that I'm barefoot or that I look like hell. I *need* to hear her say it right now.

She closes the door.

The room is no bigger than a walk-in closet with stark white walls and filing cabinets stacked next to a desk with a computer on it. A spreadsheet program is open on the computer. As Kally minimizes the screen, I spy a photo of her—the way she used to look, with that brilliant blond hair—with a little blond boy. I lift it off the desk with a trembling hand. Kally doesn't say a word, simply stands there as if she's waiting for me to go first.

She who speaks first loses.

I've already lost everything, so why not?

"He looks just like Chet." The calmness of my voice surprises me. It's as if a stand-in has stepped in and taken over my role.

"Avril, I'm so sorry…."

And the dam breaks, wracking my body with sobs for the loss and the hurt and the betrayal. For the child I so desperately wanted, but will never have.

Kally reaches out as if to touch me, but her hand hovers midair. "I—"

I jerk away from her. "I don't want your justifications or your excuses." I spit the words through my tears. "The only thing I want to know is how this happened when we lived on the other side of the country?"

She shakes her head and stares at the floor.

Even with her head bowed, I see her throat working as if she's weighing her words. When she looks up, I see the tears streaming down her cheeks.

And I think *how dare you cry…?*

"It only happened once—"

"It only happened once, and you got pregnant."

She shrugs and swipes at her face. "It was when he came home for my mother's funeral."

I do the math in my head.

Yep. Five years ago. Chet had been in the Andes filming a segment for his show and he flew straight from South America to Florida when I called to tell him Kally's mother, Caro, had passed away. He said he'd go to the funeral. To represent *us* since I was too scared to get on a plane and fly cross-country by myself. He told everyone I was in the middle of working on a movie and couldn't get away. That's why I couldn't come with him.

Lie. Lie. Lie.

That's what I get for lying. For being a coward.

I wasn't working on a movie. I was at Salon Chez Pierre over on Santa Monica Boulevard. Only my mother knew the truth. She's even better at keeping secrets than I imagined.

I stare down at the photo of the smiling boy.

"What's his name?" I ask.

"His name is Sam. Avril, it just happened. I didn't set out to seduce your husband. I was upset. Chet was holding me… Comforting me—"

"Don't you dare try to make Chet the sole villain in this story!" I fling the picture onto her desk. It slides across a pile of papers and hits the computer. "It took two. It doesn't matter whether you *intended* for it to happen or not. It

NANCY ROBARDS THOMPSON   103

happened. And no amount of explaining or apologies will change that."

She looks as if I've slapped her, which makes me want to scream.

"I was just starting to put my life back together after losing my husband. Now you've killed him all over again. And to you, it was *just one of those things*."

I've had enough. I brush past her toward the door.

"Would it be better if I told you I loved him, Avril?"

My hand freezes on the knob.

"I always did, you know. But you swooped in and took what you wanted, just like you always did. That night when he was holding me, I guess I decided for once I was going to take what I wanted. But you'll win in the end, Avril. You always did." She crosses her arms across her middle. "Always will."

I choke a little as I whirl to face her full on.

"What's left for me to win? You've taken it all. Right after Chet died, I thought I didn't have anything to live for. Now, I *know* I don't. Because you've killed every memory, every last shred of what was decent and true in my life. You have a child, Kally. Tell me, what do I have?" I hold out my hands palms up. "Nothing."

This time I do leave. Straight for a place that's dark and scary.

CHAPTER 9

Avril, wait!" Kally calls from across the parking lot.

"Leave me alone." My voice is weak and the briny wind whips my hair into my face and carries my words in the opposite direction. I wish the wind would lift me up and carry me far away from this place. If Hades wanted to drag me off today, I'd be glad to see him.

Despite the gray day, the hot pavement burns my feet, and I pick up my pace, making my way back to the beach. The only thing I can focus on is getting back to the sand and water, away from Kally and the hateful reality she just dumped on me.

"I am not letting you out of my sight after what you just said back there," she says. "I know you're hurting, and I'm so sorry for that, but it's not worth doing something stupid, Avril."

I break into a run, desperate to get away from her. I want to scream, "Haven't you done enough damage?" Just as my feet hit the sand, a big hand closes around my arm, jerking me off stride. Surfer Boy, of course, there to do Kally's bidding.

A few seconds later, she joins us, breathless and pleading.

"Avril, let me drive you home."

"Don't you even try to be nice to me."

Kally shakes her head, her eyes so full of sorrow and unshed tears, I lose it and fall to my knees in the sand. Kally does, too, and wraps her arms around me and I sob on her shoulder until it's soaked. I can't move. A strange icy-cold seeps into my bones, as if the day has turned to eternal night and there's nothing left for me in this world. Just black emptiness. The world has crumbled around my feet, I'm standing on but a sliver of surface in the midst of a void. Any false moves will send me tumbling into hell.

Maybe it wouldn't be such a bad thing to succumb. And I feel myself tumble over the edge….

I OPEN MY EYES and find myself in the backseat of a moving car. I'm crammed between a child's car seat, which claims the middle of the small space, and the window, which I'm leaning my head against.

I'm tucked behind the driver—Kally. Surfer Boy rides shotgun, presumably to ensure I don't go gonzo and cause Kally to have a wreck.

I blink—once, twice—and try to remember how I got here, not believing I could black out. But the car seat snags me.

A car seat.

For Chet's son.

My *husband's* son.

The realization causes nausea to crest in the back of my throat. Even so, my hand flexes and reaches out for the gray plastic seat, as if by touching it, I'd somehow push through this nightmare and reach Chet on the other side. There, he'd be alive and would tell me this was all a bad dream— that he'd never cheated on me, that he hadn't given my best friend the child he was supposed to give me.

Surfer Boy turns around to check on me, but I manage to close my eyes in the nick of time. Still, I can't let go of the cold, hard edge of the boy's seat. *Sam's seat.* I grip it so hard my fingernails buckle against the inflexible plastic. The harder I squeeze, the stronger the fury inside me grows.

I want to open the car door and jump out and get as far away from her and this damn gray car seat as I possibly can. Even if it means I have to walk back to California.

Or fly back.

I loosen my hold on the plastic and my hand falls to the upholstered seat.

At this precise moment, at least I have my wits about me enough to realize I'm better off staying silent rather than yelling at Kally or demanding that she pull the car over and let me out.

I curl my bare toes. They protest the action with a pain that feels as if glass is being driven into the soles of my feet. Six miles in bare feet.

I hurt all over—physically and emotionally. I'm so

drained that I don't think I could fight or walk right now even if I had to.

Well, maybe if I *had* to.

But I don't have to. And if I utter one word, Kally will surely feel compelled to talk to me—to explain away what she did. The last thing I want to do is talk to her right now.

I mean, what's there to discuss?

We've pretty much said it all.

Through half-closed eyes, I make out the familiar wooden *Welcome to Sago Beach* sign, and the businesses on Main Street. Kally makes the double left that brings us back behind the salon. I lift my head and blink at the familiar sight of home. This place where I grew up. The place where Kally spent nearly as much time as I did all those years ago.

Like everything else, *home* looks different now, too. Foreign and faraway. The thought of going inside and dealing with Mama seems almost as repugnant as staying out here and making chitchat with Kally and Surfer Boy.

But I'll take my chances inside. Maybe Mama has a late customer. She might not be home.

Yeah, right.

I suck in a deep rattling breath, lift my head off the window and try to open the door, but it won't budge.

Child locks. Of course.

"Oops, sorry." Kally pops the lock, then slides out of the

car faster than I can open my own door. Once I'm out, I don't even look at her. I just walk straight to the steps that lead to this place I used to call home.

Now, it feels empty and hollow.

"Avril?" Kally says the word to my back. I stop as if she's pinning me in place, but I don't turn around.

"Avril, I'm sorry. I wish I could tell you how sorry I really am. I know you hate me right now and I can't blame you. But after you've had a chance to…" She trails off. I hope she's choking on the words.

What? I want to ask. After I have a chance to come to terms with it? Get over it?

"After you've had a chance to digest what's happened, I want to talk to you about something."

"That's easy—no!" I spit the word without turning around. "I never want to talk to you again."

I pull open the door.

"I think you'll want to hear what I have to say." Her tone is urgent, just this side of pleading. "I think you'll find a great deal of poetic justice in what I have to tell you. Or maybe you'll interpret it as karmic payback."

Karmic payback? What the—

I whirl around and scowl at her. I can't help it. "*Umm,* gee, let me think." I put my index finger to my temple. "No. Because there's nothing that could possibly balance the scales between us, Kally. Even if I watched you suffer the same kind of slow torturing death you've put me through the karmic scales still wouldn't balance."

"You're scaring me, Avril."

"And am I supposed to care? You slept with my husband, Kally. I am officially released from caring about you."

She lifts her chin and stares up to the sky as if she's saying some sort of silent prayer.

"All this talk about karma—two wrongs don't cancel each other out. Nothing you could do or say could ever make this right. So just go back to your coffeehouse and your son, and leave me alone."

She looks as if I've hit her where it hurts, and I get a small amount of satisfaction from that.

"You're right, Avril, two wrongs never make a right, and if you've made up your mind you're never going to talk me again, I'm going to tell you this while I have the chance. About a year ago I was diagnosed with acute lymphocytic leukemia. It's advanced, and the prognosis is bad. I'm not telling you this to make excuses or to gain your pity. I just hope that later, you'll find it in your heart to listen to what I need to say to you."

I stand there stunned for a moment, watching her limp back to her car.

I'm still trying to process what she just told me when Lonnie Sue, looking pale and frantic, bursts out of the building.

"Oh, thank God, it *is* you." She throws her arms around

me and squeezes me tight. "Your mama's in the hospital. I was just about ready to send the sheriff out to find you."

A chill seeps into my bones.

"Lonnie Sue, what's wrong? What's happened to Mama?"

Lonnie Sue squeezes her eyes shut. Her face contorts. Opening her eyes, she takes my hand.

"Oh, honey, after Dani hit her, your mama smacked her head pretty hard when she fell down. About an hour after you left, she passed out cold and Gilda called the paramedics. Gilda just called from the hospital. They said something about—let me see if I get this right—a cerebral hematoma. Does that sound right? If that's what it is, she'll need surgery, sugar."

Her words knock the wind out of me.

"You and me had better get ourselves on over to the hospital."

The engine of Kally's car roars to life.

"Is that Kally? She can drive us."

"Lonnie Sue, come on. Let's take your car."

"Can't. It's broken."

Lonnie Sue runs after Kally's car. "Hey, Kally? Stop! Please! Kally!"

"What about Mama's car?" I yell.

She ignores me, but manages to get close enough to pound on the trunk. The brake lights flash, and the car slows to a stop. Lonnie Sue trots up next to the driver's side door.

"Could you please drive us to Cocoa Beach? Tess is in the hospital."

I'm floored, really. That Mama's in the hospital. That Kally's been exiled from Sago Beach since everyone put two and two together about her and Chet. She's been carrying the burden of her cancer all alone. Still, when Lonnie Sue, who was surely one of the most indignant of the bunch, asks her for a favor, Kally's right there to help.

CHAPTER 10

I run upstairs to change out of the sandy clothes, because of the uncertainty of Mama's condition, I don't waste time on a shower. The minute I step inside the apartment, I see those hateful Prada sandals sitting by the front door, shiny and clean, not a speck of sand on them.

Mama must've picked them up off the beach—was it just earlier today?

I want to kick them out of my way, but a flood of conflicting emotion stops me.

I don't want her to be nice to me.

But if something happens to her...

You'll be so racked with grief, her betrayal won't even enter into the equation. It's Persephone, pointing out the painfully obvious.

Take it from someone who's had the mother of all meddling mothers—let it go.

As I find myself in the backseat of Kally's car—*for the second time today*—I stare at my dirty feet sticking out of the pristine sandals. I try not to think about how things have slid from bad to worse since the moment I arrived.

I brace my elbows on my knees, cradle my head in my hands, and rock back and forth to the rhythm of the car wheels turning over the road's rough asphalt.

There's a cadence that seems to sing:

Bad to worse.

Bad to worse.

Bad to worse.

There's a pattern here. Bad. Worse. Rock bottom?

No. No. No.

The only way things can hit rock bottom is if Mama doesn't pull through. And that's *not* going to happen.

I can't even process what Kally told me. Leukemia? That's curable, isn't it? With all the advances in modern medicine?

I can't focus on Kally right now. So, for now, I fold up the thought and put it in a little box and store it on an out-of-the-way shelf in the back of my mind.

I feel like I'm playing a game of Russian roulette. But rather than a single bullet in this gun that is my life now, every slot but one is loaded.

A hand gives my arm a gentle squeeze, and I abruptly sit back in the seat. Lonnie Sue smiles over at me from the other side of the boy's car seat. She looks weary, flattened out. All I can do is look away, out the window at the stretches of marshland whizzing by in a blur of gold and green and brown.

Dead colors.

Cerebral hematoma.

Blood clot on the brain.

God, that's serious. Even if I wanted to be mad at my mother, a blood clot on the brain preempts any and all anger; any and all infractions or breaches of trust.

Oh, Mama…please hang on. I'm coming.

My mind keeps rehashing the last words I said to her: *Oh, for God's sake. Don't be ridiculous.*

Each beat of my heart, each *bad-to-worse thump-thump-thump* of the car's tires on the road seems like a tighter squeeze of the trigger of the loaded gun.

I lean my forehead against the window. It's cool and smooth against my skin. A touchstone, of sorts, when all of my touchstones are gone—everything I thought was real is gone or threatened—and here I sit along for the ride, help-less to do anything about anything. If something happens to my Mama—

Stop it!

Do not even go there.

I sit up straight again, strengthening my resolve. No matter how much I hate being at the mercy of anyone, I will not play the victim.

Right here, right now, this is not about me.

That thought above all sobers me.

I suck it up and drink in a long, slow fortifying breath,

reminding myself that you can find patterns in anything if you look long enough and listen hard enough.

I zone out and stare out the window at the rows of pine trees. If you catch them at just the right angle, they look like an army of soldiers standing at attention.

We pass flat stretches of land dotted with palm trees; more forests of skinny pines that give way to expanses of palmetto-laced marsh.

Real Florida.

I try to roll down my window, but it won't budge. *Child locks*.

"Will you unlock my window, please? I need some fresh air."

"Sure," says Surfer Boy.

The warm breeze roars through the open space, blocking out the monotonous dirge of tires on pavement. I lean into the humid wind and its subtle dampness seeps into my pores. Notes of green and salt and a touch of sulfur—it's decay, something primitive, back to the basics, back to square one. I lean my head out farther so the wind totally engulfs me, blowing my hair away from my face and distorting my vision so the long, black ribbon of highway stretching across the center of the flat road really does appear to lead all the way to infinity.

It used to gripe me, this long road to nowhere. This primitive no man's land. My destiny glittered somewhere out there on the horizon and I wanted whatever lay on the other side.

My destiny was with Chet, of course, and together we were bound for much greater things than this pedestrian Popsicle stand of a town.

Now, here I am back again and the only thing in the entire world I want is for my mother to be okay. I find myself making a bargain with God that if my mother will be okay, I'll find a way to look past all the other crap. Because the possibility of losing her certainly puts everything in perspective.

"I DON'T REMEMBER IF I LOCKED THE apartment door," I say as Lonnie Sue, Gilda and I sit in the hospital, waiting for word on Mama. Kally and Surfer Boy dropped us off at the emergency room entrance and left. Gilda was waiting for us and led us up to a smaller, quieter room for friends and family of patients. The room is empty except for the three of us.

"That's okay," Lonnie Sue says. "Your mama always says the day she has to start locking her door is the day she leaves Sago Beach. And I don't blame her one bit."

The three of us nod and our conversation trails off, replaced by the waiting-room television, which is broadcasting an early-evening celebrity tabloid show.

The waiting room smells of burnt coffee, though there's no coffeepot in sight, floor wax and that ominous antiseptic smell indigenous to hospitals. I'm waiting for Gilda to start in on me about my flight down the beach, but she doesn't. She just sits there quietly, holding my hand.

"You know, it's strange, this kind of makes me think of the night Caro died," says Lonnie Sue. "Us sittin' here waiting. Except Kally was here, of course. And Avril wasn't."

How might things have been different if I'd been here for Kally when her mother was dying?

Gilda shakes her head. "Sure as I'm sittin' here, Caro's turning over in her grave after what that girl's done."

They make disgusted, *tsk-tsking* sounds.

I ignore them because if I comment one way or another, I'll have to ask Gilda and Lonnie Sue how they can cast stones, when they're just as guilty for keeping from me what Kally did, as she was doing it. Basically, they're accessories to the crime.

I know. I know. It probably doesn't make sense, but right now, that's as far as I can take it. I'll sort it out later. For right now, I push it back into the far corner of my mind—on top of the pile marked *deal with it later*.

Grasping at anything to change the subject, I ask, "Why didn't we just drive Mama's car rather than having Kally drive us?"

"Gilda grabbed Tess's purse when the ambulance came thinking she'd need her insurance card and all. I asked after the keys when she called to give me an update."

"They were in Tess's handbag." Gilda pats Mama's purse, which she's cradling on her ample middle.

"And I looked all over tarnation for a spare set," says

Lonnie Sue. "But I couldn't find it. She does have a spare key to that car, doesn't she?"

"I doubt it," I say. "Or if she does, it's locked away in a safe somewhere to keep anyone from driving her beloved car."

We laugh at this because it's so my mother. Then we stop and heave a collective sigh. That's when the tears come.

"Oh, she just has to be okay."

Lonnie Sue puts her arm around me. "How much longer do you think it will be before we get word?" she asks Gilda.

"Don't know, honey." Gilda rubs my arm with her chubby hand. "How about if I go ask the nurse?"

She gets up and goes over to a glass-partitioned desk.

According to the clock on the wall, we've barely been here an hour.

Lonnie Sue sighs, uncrosses her legs and recrosses them in the other direction, kicking her top leg back and forth, a nervous tick that has every potential of driving me nuts.

If I let it. But I'm mindful of the bargain I made with God.

We sit quietly for a long time, until Gilda returns with the news that the nurse will let us know as soon as she hears something.

"Well, that could be next Christmas if they go on hospital time." Lonnie Sue shifts in her chair and stretches and yawns.

Her cell phone rings and as she fishes it out of her pocket, Gilda says, "Didn't you see the sign over there? You're supposed to silence that thing."

Lonnie Sue swats at Gilda's words as if they're a gnat buzzing in her personal space and flips open her phone. "Hello? Oh, hey, Sid, honey."

Lonnie Sue sits up straighter, pressing her shoulders back, which makes her boobs stick out.

Man-alert posture, which confirms my inkling that Lonnie Sue's playing a little hanky panky with Sid Olsen. Then again, Lonnie Sue usually has several rounds of hanky panky going at once—sort of like a continuous hanky panky hokey pokey.

She puts her hand over the mouthpiece and whispers to us, "It's the sheriff calling to check on Tess." Then she says to him, "Well, aren't you the sweetest thing to call. I just told Avril you were checking in on her Mama. No, we haven't heard yet. Tess is having some kind of brain scan, and we're waiting for her doctor to come out and tell us exactly what he finds…. Yes…." Lonnie Sue slants a glance at me and the way she says, "Umm-hold on a sec," and then gets up and walks out of the room, I guess that Sid asked about my disappearing act earlier today.

But I'm too worried about Mama to feel awkward or irritated by the probability of them discussing my actions and motivations, playing judge and jury about whether I was justified to flee or if my actions are partially to blame for Mama being in the hospital.

Plus, Kally and Surfer Boy walk into the waiting room with a cardboard tray of foam cups and a white bag.

She offers Gilda the coffee tray—which, to my great relief, Gilda accepts— and hands the bag to me.

"I thought you might be hungry," she says.

Kally turns and, clinging to Surfer Boy's arm for support, limps out the way she came in.

"Thank you," I murmur to her back. But she doesn't turn around.

Are you watching this, God? I'm trying. I'm trying very hard. Can you please send me some good news about my mother?

Gilda hands me one of the cups as a tall man in green scrubs walks in.

"Are you Mrs. Mulligan's daughter?"

I nod, trying to interpret his blank face.

"I'm Hal Landvik, your mother's attending physician."

CHAPTER 11

"You're going to be okay, Mama." She looks so small and fragile lying there in the hospital bed hooked up to all those tubes and monitors. My heart compresses. "I was so worried about you."

I brush a strand of red hair off her forehead. My fingers linger as I smile down at her.

She grabs my hand, pulling it down to her side, and squeezes. Her touch is comforting. "I've got a hard head, baby."

"I'll say." Lonnie Sue laughs.

"Well, a concussion is nothing to sneeze at, but it's a far cry from a cerebral hematoma," says Gilda.

Mama waves away the words. "It was just a little bump on the head. I don't see why I can't go home."

"You passed out, Mama. The doctor wants to keep you overnight for observation. Don't give them a hard time."

She pulls her hand out of mine and rests the crook of her arm over her eyes. "Honey, I am so sorry you found out about Kally the way you did. I never meant—"

"We'll talk later." I push down a sick feeling as thoughts

of Chet and Kally—together—try to crowd in. "Right now you need to rest."

She lifts her arm to frown at me and makes noises like she's going to protest, but I silence her with a preempting hand. "Just go to sleep. I'll be back to pick you up tomorrow."

"She's right, Tess," says Gilda. "You need to take it easy. The only way you're going to rest is if we leave. So, come on, girls, let's get out of here and leave her be."

For some reason when we're crossing the parking lot to Gilda's car, I think about Kally slipping away before we rushed up to Mama's room. Isn't that how it usually happens? You're distracted by something and a person who at one time meant the world to you just slips away....

PERCEPTION AND REALITY aren't absolute, you know. They change, chameleonlike, depending on what they're touching, who they're touching. Forthright to devious. Sunny to cloudy. Yes, the range of emotions run a vicious cycle. Just when you think you've got it all figured out, reason morphs and changes, scattering what seemed to be the perfect answer like sand in a gust of wind.

That night, I mostly toss and turn, adrift on a sea of ugliness. Morning takes its own sweet time reporting for work, but the night finally brings the dawn, and dawn brings the day.

I get up and dress in shorts, a plain pink pullover and tennis shoes.

I sit on the side of the twin bed—the same bed I slept in all the years I was growing up—and glance around my room. It looks the same as I left it all those years ago. The same pink walls, same white and gold-trimmed desk; same movie posters and pictures of my favorite stars on the wall. It strikes me that Mama never changed it. She could've turned it into an office, a yoga studio or a sewing room.

Of course, she doesn't sew or do yoga, but she could've made it her own. Rather than making it a shrine to my youth, since I hardly ever came home.

The last time I sat here, my future looked bright and shiny. I was going to be a star. This is *not* the role in which I thought fate would cast me.

Sitting here in my old room, on the edge of my old bed, it's as if destiny has picked me up and deposited me back in time; it's like destiny reached back, searching for what it originally created—taking forms, shapes, and textures from the past—and molded them into something resembling my old life, but it's totally out of context.

Last night I lay here in this room tossing and turning, telling myself this revelation about Chet and Kally having a child is so huge, I'm either going to totally lose it and tumble headfirst over the edge or I'll calmly gather my wits.

There doesn't seem to be much middle ground.

But yesterday seems foggy and dim, as if everything happened years ago. Still it's just been one day. I figure I should cut myself some slack.

I walk down to the beach to watch the rising sun paint a gorgeous picture across the eastern sky: cotton candy clouds dance across brush strokes of Dreamsicle and concord grape, finally burning off to a cloudless, impossibly clear blue.

There are days in Sago Beach when the light is so pure and the azure sky hangs so low over the water it's as if you can reach up and claim heaven like a prize.

Today is one of those days. The sun draws diamonds and casts prisms on the sea. It's so beautiful it's like a mistake after yesterday's journey to hell and back. I sit in the sand, scribbling lines and squiggles while contemplating the dichotomy: I whisper a prayer of thanks that Mama's okay, and recall my vow to "get past" all the other crap. There's so much of it, I don't even know where to start. Kally and Chet? The child? Kally's leukemia? What will become of the child if…?

It just seems wrong for the day to be so beautiful with all these emotional clouds hanging overhead; as wrong as it seems for me to give in to these terrible feelings that threaten to push through the steel cell in which I've cast them.

The salt wind stings my eyes; I taste and smell the very essence of life in the air. A gull circles overhead *cawing*, a white streak on the brilliant sky. It sounds as if the heavens are looking down and laughing, goading me to wallow in all the things that I shouldn't give in to right now.

To be mad at my mother who, at one point yesterday, I feared was knocking on death's door; to be furious at Lonnie Sue and Gilda and Dani and the whole of Sago Beach for keeping such a secret; to hate Kally and Chet for the ultimate betrayal—but haven't they both been punished enough?

I suppose if I was honest, Chet and I not only grew apart when we moved to California, we also grew up and became two totally different people.

Would our marriage have lasted in the face of such differences—him loving his taste of fame while I felt as if I was riding his wake on good days, while on all the others I was simply in the way?

Long before Kally, he and I were on a collision course with disaster.

Horrible, gnawing grief doubles me over, stealing my breath as it draws out my tears like it's going for blood.

I sit there with my head in my hands, fighting the guilt and anger and bile churning inside me, until the first licks of high tide roll in, erasing the lines and squiggles I've etched in the sand, as if it's trying to rub out any and all traces that I'd been here. But the water doesn't touch me. It laps around me and rolls out to sea, barely missing me.

You know, says Persephone, *you're caught in an emotional undertow. If you keep fighting, you're gonna go under; you'll be swept into the sea of your grief.*

What was it that they used to say about getting caught in the

undertow? Relax. Swim sideways. Stay parallel to the shore
until the current loosens its bully grip.

You're going to have to swim sideways through these feelings
for a while before you'll know what to do. But if you keep fighting
them, you'll go under.

Rogue thoughts pull at me: Everyone knew but me.
Mama knew. My own mother knew, but didn't tell me.

It's the first pull of the current, says Persephone, *but it's a*
starting point.

I know she's right. As much as I hate to admit it.

So I stand, a little unsteady on my feet, and start walking—swimming parallel to my grief, keeping my head above
the pain and anger, trying to work up the strength to swim
away.

I COULD WALK FOR HOURS on the beach. The only problem
is once you realize how far you've walked, you have to turn
around and cover the same distance back. I decide to take
a detour, thinking a change of scenery will help. I veer off
at the first boardwalk past the stretch of beach that runs
parallel to downtown Sago Beach, figuring I'll walk up this
way and loop back around toward home. I have to pick up
Mama at one o'clock and since I'm not wearing a watch, I
figure this is probably the smartest plan.

The long wooden path leads from the beach, over the
dunes and through some palmetto scrub until it dumps out

at Holland Park, which has showers, picnic tables, parking and beach access for the general public.

During the summer it's packed with locals and tourists alike, but right now the sandy parking lot is deserted except for a skinny, brown mutt of a dog sniffing around the empty garbage cans, looking a little displaced. When the animal sees me, he comes bounding over, every part of his body wiggling as if to say, *Oh, thank God you're here. Now my day is complete.*

I glance around to see if her owners are around, but see no one. Squatting down, I give the animal a few strokes. No collar or tags.

"What's the matter, girl? Are you looking for breakfast? Slim pickings around here this time of year, huh?"

The dog barks, as if to ask, *What do you have for me?*

"Sorry, I wasn't even smart enough to eat breakfast myself before I started out this morning, much less bring something for a friend."

I stand, my knees cracking with the movement. "Well, good luck. I hope you hit the jackpot."

I turn to go, but the dog barks and runs up alongside of me, trotting along. I start to shoo her away, but then I figure, what's the harm? She'll eventually get bored and wander off.

Go back to where she belongs.

When I exit the park and turn onto A1A, she's still keeping up with me as if she and I set out on this journey together. In a strange sort of way, I enjoy her quiet company. Every time

I glance down, she's looking up with a lolling tongue and soulful, brown eyes that—crazy as it seems—are comforting. In turn, this makes me realize for the span of a few minutes in her company, I— Well, I can't exactly say I forgot my problems, but I suppose I was momentarily distracted.

Even though the beach is deserted, A1A is a major thoroughfare and is busy no matter what time of day or night. As cars whiz past, I begin to worry that this might not be the safest place for a dog. If she got hurt because she was following me…

I squat down and scratch her behind the ears.

"Do you have a family?"

She cocks her head to the right as if she's trying to understand what I'm saying, then makes a sound that's not quite a bark, but more like a yodel.

"No? No family? Except for my mother, who I'm really mad at right now, I'm pretty much on my own, too."

A car blows by a little too close to us. It makes a *whooshing* sound. Another honks as it sails by.

"Crazy drivers. Come on, girl this is no place for you to wander. Let's get you somewhere safer."

I pick her up and wait a few moments for a clear stretch, then cut over to the west of A1A, to a tree-lined street that's not quite so busy.

She lies in my arms, panting and relaxed. I'm surprised how contented she is, and how she lets me hold her while we walk.

Once I'm sure we're out of harm's way, I set her down, but she continues to follow me. We happen upon a neat little row of houses, some with white picket fences around them, others with nice manicured lawns. They look as if they've been recently refurbished. The neighborhood is about two miles outside of Sago Beach. Even though it's close, it's a different world from Sago Beach proper. Not that the residents wouldn't be welcome to shop at the hardware store, do business at the bank or have their hair done at Tess's Tresses, but these people aren't woven into the fabric of my life.

They're sort of like the Dolce & Gabbana jeans and Prada sandals I got used to in L.A. compared to the Wranglers and Keds I grew up wearing.

Most houses have nice, newer-model cars in the driveway. I would imagine a good number of the residents make decent money working as engineers and scientists at the Space Center.

Even so, I doubt the modern world and all its outsiders could eclipse Sago Beach.

A woman in a suit walks out of the last house on the left. She picks up her newspaper and gets into her BMW.

She drives by and doesn't wave.

She'd make a great neighbor.

The yellow bungalow on the corner has a For Rent sign in the lawn. There are no cars in the driveway, and I can tell by the way that the blinds sit wide open that the house is empty. I walk up and let myself inside the white wooden gate. The dog trots along beside me.

I lean in over the hedge for a glimpse inside the window. From this vantage point, I can see a small living room with hardwood floors.

"What do you think?" I ask the dog.

She squats and pees in the yard then runs in a wide circle before she drops and starts rolling in the grass.

"I know. I like it, too." I bend down and stroke her head. She pants her appreciation, her adoring eyes watching my every move.

"So what do you say? Want to live here? Want to be roommates?"

CHAPTER 12

There are two sides to every story—and somewhere in the middle lies the truth.

I remind myself of this as Mama rattles off a litany of reasons for not leveling with me, while I drive her home from the hospital. That same Patsy Cline CD is playing. This time she's singing "I Fall To Pieces." As I turn off the player, I make a mental note to buy Mama some new music.

"Oh, baby, you were trying to get pregnant and I didn't want to upset you. I thought once you had your baby, well, the truth would come easier—"

"That's rich, Mama. Absolutely rich." I don't want to fight with her, but the words bubble up and out of my mouth before I can stop them. "How can you say that? We've known for the past four years that I can't conceive."

Guilt and anger coalesce into raw, stabbing grief. I know where the conversation will lead—

"Oh, honey, after Chet's accident, I couldn't bring myself to tell you. What good would it have done? I mean, think about it. Would it have solved anything?"

I keep my eyes on the road and a death-grip on the steering wheel. Not just because it was like pulling teeth to get her permission to drive her precious car. The doctor had to step in and say he wouldn't release her unless someone else drove. But I keep my eyes on the road because I don't want to look at Mama right now, all black and blue and earnest.

She sighs and starts clicking the metal clasp on her purse. "I never knew for sure—" Her voice breaks. She clears her throat. "What if it wasn't true? Was I supposed to stir up a hornet's nest not knowing with one hundred percent certainty whether Chet was the father of Kally's baby?"

I pound the steering wheel with my right fist. "All you have to do is take one look at that boy to know that Chet was the father."

"I never saw the boy, Avril. Honest to God. Once people started talking she moved over to Cocoa and for all I know she hasn't set foot back in these parts since."

I stop at a red light and force myself to look at her. She closes her eyes and leans her head back against the headrest, looking just this side of dead. The horror-thought occurs to me that she might not be able to handle this confrontation. I mean, *really* not be able to deal with it.

So why are you pushing it? Persephone says. *She's said she's sorry. What more do you want? She can't go back and undo the past. For that matter, you can't go back and undo it, either. Are you going to keep chewing on it until it turns you into a hard, bitter old lady?*

Give me a break. I'm still trying to digest it, I think.

Yeah, well, I'm just saying, quips Persephone.

Mama and I ride quietly for the rest of the fifteen-minute trip back to the apartment.

When we get there, Dani, of all people, is sitting on the steps outside petting the dog, which I tied up on the porch to keep her from wandering around A1A. Dani stands when she sees the car, wringing her hands, looking tired and anxious.

"Oh, dear." Mama slides down in the seat a little and presses her right hand to the side of her face. She's not an animal lover, but I'm pretty sure she isn't reacting to the dog. In fact, I don't think she even saw the animal. What I can't figure out is if she's trying to hide from Dani or if the sheer magnitude of another potential confrontation weighs her down.

Still, judging by the contrite look on Dani's face—her hunched shoulders and bowed head—she's obviously here to make amends, not to pick another fight.

I pull the car into the covered space across the street, shove it in Park and turn off the ignition. The old faithful T-Bird ticks and pings, as if it's clucking its tongue and saying, *Do something. Get rid of Dani.*

"Wait here," I finally say. "I'll tell her you're not up to company right now."

When I start to get out of the car, Mama puts a hand on

my elbow. "No, I'd best talk to her now. Might as well get it over with. The longer we stew, the harder it'll be to get to the other side of this mess."

Her words hit home.

"Are you sure?" I ask.

She nods and slides out the open door.

I stay in the car with the door open, not quite sure what to say to Dani, even though I'm sure she didn't come to see me.

In the rearview mirror, I see her take a few tentative steps toward Mama. I hear her faint southern drawl....

"Oh my God, Tess. I am so, so sorry—" She chokes, then bursts into tears, probably devastated by the bruises on Mama's face.

And she should be.

My mother stands silent for a moment. In profile, her mouth is a tightly drawn line, a contrast to her swollen face. She holds out her arms to Dani.

"It's okay, honey."

Dani swipes at her tears and then hugs my mother, like a sinner coming home. She sobs into her shoulder and rambles incoherently. The only words I recognize through the storm of anguish are *sorry, forgive me, never drink again* and something about Gilda and Lonnie Sue.

"Hush now, we're all gonna be okay." Mama pats Dani's back. "We're *all* gonna be okay."

I feel small cowering in the car. Small and angry at Dani

for causing all this, for hitting my mother, for spilling the beans about Chet the way she did.

If your mama can forgive Dani for giving her a concussion, what right do you have to stay mad at anyone? says Persephone.

I blink against the cresting pain that's becoming all too familiar and stand up, hoping to shake the ensuing nausea.

Mama's hurting. Dani's hurting. I'm hurting. In moments of Zen-like clarity, I realize even Kally is suffering. We're all reeling from the hard landing in this twisted, screwed-up place fate has dropped us.

Since I've never been very Zen-like, I suppose the art of forgiveness is not something I'll master overnight. These are uncharted seas I have yet to traverse—deep, dark, stormy waters that lurk beyond the cays of my raw emotion.

Dani spies me over Mama's shoulder. Her tearstained face contrite, she looks so beaten down, like the only reason she's standing is because she's simply too worn out to fall down. "Avril, I don't know how in the world you can ever forgive me."

She pauses expectantly, like she's waiting for me to join Mama in the *We're all fine now* chorus, but I don't. All I can do is stand there, mutely looking at her looking at me.

Mama turns toward me, keeping an arm around Dani. She's choosing sides. She shoots me a you-can-jump-in-any-time look and this irritates me. It's fine if she chooses to forgive and forget, but my train doesn't run on her schedule. In fact, I'm not completely fine with *her* yet.

I need a little time.

To process everything. Sure I promised to get past the anger, but I can't just flip a switch.

Finally, Dani breaks the silence. "Avril, I was drunk. I'm not gonna drink anymore. I swear it."

She shrugs and bows her head again.

Woof. The deep, guttural bark emanates from the porch.

"What in the world was that?" Mama glances around. The little dog I'd met on my walk stands up—*Woof. Woof-woof-woof-woof*—and strains at the confines of the rope that secures her. Before I went and got Mama, I bathed her using the hose and some shampoo from the salon.

"Why is there a dog tied to my porch?"

Woof. Woof-woof-woof-woof.

I walk over and her skinny brown body wiggles all over.

"She followed me home when I went out for my walk this morning." I bend down and scratch her behind her ears, and she tries to lick my face. She smells like the apple-scented shampoo I used on her.

Dani looks uncertain, as if she doesn't quite know what to say. Mama looks horrified, as if she fears the animal's next move will be to squat and poop on the steps.

"She followed you home. And you tied her up on my porch." Mama's voice is flat, and she quirks an auburn brow at me, then at Dani, like she's trying to figure out if this is a conspiracy. But ultimately, she turns back to me. "What, may I ask, are you planning to do with—" she flutters her fingers at the dog "—it?"

"I'm going to post notices and if no one claims her, I'll keep her."

She shakes her head.

"No. Oh, no. Avril, honey, I'm sorry, but that dog *cannot* stay here. This apartment is not big enough." She makes a face. "*Oooh*, just thinking of all the dirt and bugs on that thing makes my skin crawl."

She crosses her arms and rubs the sleeves of her bright green blouse as if she's trying to brush off dog cooties. Shaking her head emphatically, she makes a face like the very thought is enough to infect her with rabies or some other nasty, animal-borne disease.

Don't get me wrong. My mother is a loving, caring person. Generous to the point of silly with forgiveness and her resources. She'd give her last dime to someone she cares about. But as far back as I can remember, Tess Mulligan never, under any circumstances, had a soft spot for animals and their fleas, dander and stinky bodily functions.

My mama was in the beauty business. She had no use for animals and the dirty, ugly messes they made.

Whining, the little dog rears up on her hind legs and puts her front paws on my leg, as if urging me to be her advocate.

Dani breaks the silence. "Well, I guess I'll go inside and get back to work."

"Honey, you look worn out," Mama says, not removing her gaze from the dog. "If you need to take another day, that's fine."

"No." Dani edges up the steps and passes me, headed toward the door. "I think working is just the medicine I need right now. I'll go in and fix my face. I'll be fine."

She shoots me a hesitant *good luck* glance and murmurs, "Avril, thank you for not telling me to go to hell," before she leaves me alone to face down Mama, who is now standing arms akimbo like she really means business.

"Avril Marie, you can't—"

"I *know*, Mama."

She looks relieved. But oh, my God, I'm ten years old again, dragging in another stray that I know in my heart of hearts I'll never get to keep. I never even had a goldfish growing up, but the need to nurture kept me trying.

"All rightie, then," Mama says. Her words pour out on a gale of victorious relief. "I'll go in and call Bucky Farley and ask him if he can load the mutt up in the back of his truck and take him over to the pound. That's probably the first place someone would look for a missing dog anyway."

As she tentatively edges toward the door, I hold the rope tight to keep the dog from jumping on her. Still, Mama glances warily at the mongrel as if she'll break loose and tear her to pieces.

I'm struck by the absurdity of how readily she forgave

Dani for pummeling her, but is so repulsed by this harmless little dog.

"Mama, don't call Bucky."

She pauses inside the door, peeking around it like it's her shield. "Don't be silly. How else are we going to get that... that thing to the pound?"

"Mama, I'm keeping it."

A FEW MINUTES LATER we're sitting on the couch looking at each other. The room looks exactly the same as it always has, only different, as if I'm looking at it underwater. I'm trying to figure out the best way to tell her I'm moving out.

"Well, I'm glad we've patched things up with Dani." She always does this—changing the subject when there's something heavy we need to discuss. "I'm glad we can put all this ugliness behind us."

I can't quite tell if that's a statement or a question. Either way, with Dani coming back to work today, it will free me up to go see the house.

"Good. I have an errand to run this afternoon and since Dani can take her own clients, I was hoping you wouldn't mind if I take the afternoon off."

"Are you going shopping? If so, why don't you wait until tonight and I'll go with you?"

"Mama, I've found a place."

The expression on her battered face avalanches to confusion.

"Come on, it's best this way. My furniture is in storage. And you know I can't live with you permanently. Staying with you was just a temporary arrangement, which I've appreciated very much."

"Avril, it's only been three days. One of which I spent in the hospital. I haven't even had a chance to sit down with you to have a civil conversation without the entire town butting in to ask if Julia Roberts wears hair extensions."

Her eyes tear up.

"Oh, Mama, wait a minute. Don't cry. Please. Let's put this into perspective. I'm moving down the road less than a mile. You make it sound like I'm moving back to California. Which, I'll be honest, thanks to the three-ring circus that's happened since I arrived, I've considered."

She makes a wailing sound.

"I'm not moving back to California." I put my hand on top of hers. "I'm staying here."

"You're doing this—because you're mad at me? You *are* mad at me, aren't you? You're punishing me."

I roll my eyes. "If I wanted to punish you, I *would* move back to California." She winces, recoils a bit. My tone sounds a lot more flippant than I'd intended.

I take a deep breath, reel in my sarcasm.

"I'm *not* trying to punish you. But to be honest, I need

some time to process everything that's happened. I don't want to be mad at you. I don't want to blame you. Or Dani or Gilda or Lonnie Sue or…"

Kally?

I can't bring myself to include her in the lineup.

"Pinning blame is not going to change a thing," I say. "But— my God, things have been going from bad to worse since I got here. Can't you understand why I need a little space? A place of my own?"

Mama swipes at a tear, straightens her shoulders and sets her jaw. But she doesn't answer me.

"Well, I suppose I'd better get downstairs and see what trouble those girls are causing now."

Her voice is cool. I can tell she's hurt.

And I'm sorry, but right now this is something I have to do.

CHAPTER 13

After Mama goes downstairs, I venture outside and sit on the steps next to the dog. As I stroke her, the mutt looks up at me and pants contentedly.

"Wait here just a little longer, okay? I'm going to check on our house now."

By this time, I figure the girls will be in a full-fledged fuss over Mama. I hope once she has a chance to distance herself, she'll feel a little better about my moving out.

Earlier this afternoon on the way to pick Mama up, I called Jennifer Rigby at Sago Beach Realty and told her I'd like to stop by. Since I had no idea how long it would take to get Mama discharged—whether she'd be ready or if her doctor would need to see her again or talk to me about special instructions—I couldn't set an appointment. So she said to call before I came to make sure she was in the office.

I take my cell out of my purse and dial her number again.

"Sago Beach Realty, Jennifer speaking. How may I help you?"

"Hi, Jennifer, it's Avril Carson. Will you be in the office in, say, the next ten minutes?"

"I will, but I have an appointment in an hour. If you come right now, that should give us plenty of time to see the house."

I shove my purse strap on my shoulder, gather the file folder containing all the financial records Jen told me I'd need to rent the place and head out the door.

DID YOU EVER NOTICE how most of the time people follow your lead? If you're delivering questionable news and you frame it in an upbeat way, generally the rest of the world smiles along with you.

After signing the lease, I decide to go straight to the beauty shop to share my *good news*.

Putting on my happy face, I open the salon's back door and slip into the familiar smell of coffee, perm solution and Lonnie Sue's looming musky perfume.

This scene I'm witnessing from the wings could be just another day in the life I left so long ago. It's as if I'm watching a rerun of a movie I've seen hundreds of times. The hum of idle chatter mingles with a quiet country tune drifting from the boom box. Gilda touches up Crystal Jones's inky color. Dani sweeps up hair off the floor and talks to Charis Harding and Maybell Jennings—with whom she seems to be on good enough terms after what happened the other day. Mama cashes out a customer I don't recognize.

Lonnie Sue—where is she? Nowhere in sight, but she could be over at the Sago Diner getting everyone a midday round of sodas, or outside smoking a cigarette, or in the back room gossiping about the latest juicy tidbit she'd heard from a customer today.

Tess's Tresses has always been Sago Beach's great gossip clearing house. The devoted ladies of Sago Beach come here like it's their house of worship.

When I left, all those years ago, my mother's beauty shop felt dull and dipped in sludgy bleakness. Like buildup on hair, it was an existence you couldn't do a thing with.

Living in such a small town seemed suffocating. Downright claustrophobic. Bored and restless, I longed to experience what lay on the other side of the horizon.

As much as I loved Chet, my greatest fear was if we stayed in Sago Beach I'd be defined by marriage and motherhood. My world would be the four walls of this salon. I wanted to be a star.

Not that I was averse to marriage and motherhood—I always wanted kids and I couldn't imagine my life without Chet, but our life had to be staged somewhere far more exciting than here and motherhood was supposed to come after I'd taken Hollywood by storm.

I guess when you're young and immortal, you can afford to believe you can script your own happily ever after. Then one day you wake up and realize that the horizon is a mirage and building a life on those stardust dreams is far from what you thought it would be.

Since I've been back I've wondered if maybe the life lesson I'm being taught is that I can never escape myself. No matter where I run, like it or not, maybe my destiny is tethered to this place that I tried so hard to get away from.

"Well, look who's here." Gilda's voice is almost mocking. Every head in the salon swivels toward me.

"Come over here, sugar," she says. "You and me need to have a little talk."

She holds up plastic-glove-covered hands smeared with hair dye the color of midnight. I take a few tentative steps into the salon, feeling as if I'm walking into enemy territory.

"Why on earth are you doing this to your mama?"

I shoot a curious glance at my mother, who doesn't look at me so much as look past me, her lips pressed into a tight line. Her customer stares at me with wide eyes. Dani clutches her broom; Maybell and Charis virtually lick their lips over this juicy tidbit; and Crystal, looking like a muddy-headed kewpie doll, swivels the chair around so that she doesn't miss anything.

"Excuse me?" Suddenly, I feel a tad defensive.

Gilda doesn't bother turning the chair back. Instead, she steps around Crystal to section off another part of hair with the pointed nozzle of the plastic dye bottle.

"What is this about you renting a house over there across A1A?" Gilda demands.

The audience gasps, glances at Mama, who looks hurt.

Gilda squirts on some color and smoothes it out with her free hand.

When I was a child, Gilda was the only person, other than Mama, who could get away with disciplining me. If I was in deep, they'd tag-team me. I have the distinct feeling the throw-down is coming and soon I'll be kissing the mat.

"Gilda, I am thirty-five years old. And as much as I love and respect you, I do not have to answer to you."

I shouldn't have said it, but I couldn't stop myself. The words erupted like a volcano in a bad B movie.

Oh, for that matter, I probably shouldn't have come here. I should've gone straight over to the house and—and what? Sat in the middle of the cold, empty floor and stared at a blank wall?

Yes, probably so. I don't want to fight. I'm so darn tired of fighting.

Lonnie Sue comes in the front door and stops in her tracks as soon as she hits the wall of tension.

"What's going on?" she asks.

"Nothing. Absolutely nothing." I start toward the back door.

"Hold on there, Ms. High and Mighty, you'd just better cool your jets." My hand is on the doorknob when Gilda's words hit. "This attitude of yours is not going to fly around here. If your Mama and Dani can forgive and forget, you can certainly do the same."

What the—?

I'm so stunned I turn around. Mama frowns at me and raises her eyebrows, making it clear she couldn't have said it better herself. Dani looks like a frightened deer and Lonnie Sue and the rest of the customers just looks back and forth among each other, Mama, Gilda and me.

"Oh, no," I say. "No. No. No! You do not get to turn this around on me."

Lonnie Sue edges toward the front desk, where she grabs a piece of paper and waves it like a white flag.

"Oh, hey, Avril. I've got a phone message for you. That sexy hunk of man named Max called you this morning and wants you to call him back."

"Thanks, but—" I shake my head, not wanting to add more fuel to Maybell, Crystal and Charis's gossip bonfire.

"Oh, come on y'all," Lonnie Sue says. "She's a grown woman. Just let her be."

Any other time, I would've deeply appreciated her taking my side, but the way Mama and Gilda are glaring at me makes me want to throw something at them.

Instead, I do the next best thing. "Maybe it's not too late to change my mind." I open the door and start to walk out, but I stop and turn back around. "Maybe I should move back to California."

THE HOUSE IS AN OLD restored Key West-style bungalow, built in the 1920s. It's yellow. A happy color. That's what I like about it. I'm going to get a little happy in my life even if I have to lease it for a while.

Standing on the front porch of my new house, I feel like a heel for threatening Mama like that in front of all the customers. Granted, Gilda brought it on. She had no right to butt in, but still—

How can the very people you love with every fiber of your being make you so crazy?

The dog, who still doesn't have a name, follows me into the empty house. The *click-click* of her claws on the hardwood living room floor echoes and makes me feel sad and displaced. It's almost like I'm homesick, but I *am* home. Or am I? I feel as if I'm caught in a strange purgatory.

California was never home.

While Sago Beach *once* was, it's…*different* now.

Yes, *different.* I'll leave it at that.

I pull the box containing Chet's ashes out of my tote bag and look around the empty house for a place to put them.

Definitely not on the fireplace mantel.

Not on the kitchen counter. I stare down at the heavy box.

"I know exactly where you belong," I say to my husband. "After what you did, you're sleeping in the guest room."

That way, I won't have to look at him all the time and remember everything that's happened. Yeah, as if out-of-sight, out-of-mind will make it easier to forget.

Once he's stowed away on the closet shelf in the extra bedroom, the dog and I plop down in the middle of the living room floor. She waits for me to get settled, then lies next to me, rolling over so her back presses against my side. As if she's too exhausted to move another inch, she sighs and looks up at me without raising her head.

"I know how you feel, girl."

I stare at the ceiling, wondering how in the world I'm going to get my furniture out of storage. I can rent a truck, that's not the problem. It's the manpower.

I suppose I could call Bucky Farley and Tim Dennison to help—and I'm sure they would, but even that seems too complicated right now.

Fatigue pulses through my body. No doubt the toll of the sleepless night. Everything always seems worse when I'm tired. Sometimes so much so that the world feels as if it's ending. Then once I'm rested, the worry never seems as insurmountable as it did.

I reach out and stroke the dog's coarse fur and feel her slow, contented breaths. Following her lead, I close my eyes.

I guess now that I have a roof over my head, there's really no rush to get my things....

THE DOG'S SHARP YELPS jolt me awake.

Knockknockknock.

There's the sound of her claws sliding across the wood and someone pounding on the door.

I sit up quickly and blink a couple of times in the dim light before I get my bearings and remember where I am.

Oh, that's right.

As I walk to the front door, I glance at my watch. *Six-thirty.*

My, gosh. I must have slept for a couple of hours. The light filtering in through the half-drawn blinds has changed from bald afternoon brightness to the softer amber glow of early evening.

I flip on the porch light and open the door.

"Surprise!" sing my Mama, Gilda, Dani and Lonnie Sue in unison.

Their arms are full of covered dishes, grocery sacks, folding chairs and even a drooping philodendron.

"This is the Sago Beach welcome wagon," says Lonnie Sue. "We brought dinner. And lawn furniture."

They sweep in and beeline for the kitchen. I suppose a little part deep inside me knew it would be them—or at least my mother. Or at least I'd hoped it would be.

I smile. "You crazy people."

They laugh and all talk at once as they empty bags and set out food on the countertops for a feast. It's as if what happened earlier never happened at all.

And I'm glad.

"Honey, I am so sorry." Gilda takes my hands in hers. "I was way out of line today—"

"Gilda, *shhh*."

She swallows hard, emotion welling up in her dark eyes. "Well, here then, hug my neck and let's not have another word about it."

"That sounds like a plan."

After she gives me a squeeze, it's Mama's turn.

"I suppose having you a mile down the road is better than on the other side of the country." She winks at me. "You need your own place. Especially if you're going to start taking in stray animals."

She bends down and pets the dog on the head—it's a short, perfunctory pat, but nonetheless, a gesture of peace. The dog wags her tail in response. "I brought you some food, too. Dog Chow. Is that okay?"

She straightens a little slowly and holds her arms out to me.

"Come here, baby. I'd rather let this dog sleep in my bed than fight with you."

We laugh, and as she hugs me tight, a tidal wave of emotion splashes over me. As long as I have these women in my life I'll be able to withstand anything.

I feel a pang at the empty spot that Kally used to fill and I wonder when I should tell them about her leukemia. Surely they don't know or they'd have told me. Even after all that's happened, they couldn't cast her out in her time of need.

Tonight, I decide as Mama kisses me on the cheek and steps back. I'll talk to them about Kally's illness tonight.

"I hope you're hungry," Dani says. "We brought a feast."

We put Gilda's unbaked casserole into the oven and the rest of the food and disposable dinnerware out on the counters.

"Good grief, y'all. There's enough here for at least ten more people."

Mama and Gilda exchange a glance.

"What?" I ask.

Lonnie Sue squeals. "Weeeell…we are expecting a couple more. I called Max and he and a friend will be here in a bit with a truck to help move your furniture from storage."

CHAPTER 14

"You called Max?" I ask. Even saying the words ties my stomach in a knot.

Lonnie Sue nods and helps herself to a cookie from a plate that Gilda just set on the counter.

"Why did you do that?" I try to keep my voice neutral. If meddling were an Olympic sport, these women would always bring home the gold.

"I figure a good way to see what a man's made of is to call and ask him to do you a tiny little favor." She stuffs the rest of the cookie in her mouth and chews, her jaws puffed out like a chipmunk.

"Moving is hardly a *tiny little favor*," I say.

Lonnie Sue continues on as if she hasn't heard me. "I don't know about you, but I want a man who's willing to roll up his sleeves and work *hard* for his reward."

"Reward? I don't know about that," I say. "But before I get involved to the point of handing out *rewards*, a man is going to have to chase me around the block and back again to collect."

Lonnie Sue's eyes shine. "Sugar, you're a natural. They love it when you play hard to get. I would offer to take care of any and all *rewards*, but I'm happy to report that things with Sid and me are going pretty good."

Lonnie Sue starts to swipe another cookie and Gilda swats her hand.

"Those are for dessert. If you eat them now, not only will you spoil your appetite, but we won't have any left for the end of the meal."

Lonnie Sue rolls her eyes. "You see, she's an equal-opportunity mother. If you're still harboring any traces of a grudge over her bossing you this afternoon, you can see it's nothing personal."

"You're darn right." Gilda winks at me, and I offer my best *no-grudge-here* smile. As soon as she turns her back to talk to Mama, Lonnie Sue takes another cookie.

At exactly seven o'clock, there's a knock on the door. Everyone looks at me.

"Prompt," says Dani.

"Answer it," Mama says.

As I make my way to the door, it's so stupid how I'm feeling—all jittery and nervous. *Oh, come on*, says Persephone, *he's just a guy. Albeit a very tall, broad-shouldered, good-looking guy. But he's just come to do you a favor. No strings attached. Just a guy who's willing to drop everything and come at the spur of the moment to move your furniture.*

In response, I think, he either has no life, or some ulterior motive that's going to leave him awfully disappointed.

Twilight is giving way to darkness and I turn on the over-head light in the living room, take a deep breath and open the door. On the porch is Max and another strong-looking, able-bodied man.

Max takes off his hat. "Good evening." It's the same black Stetson he was wearing on the plane when I met him. "Did someone call for a mover?"

"Hi, Max." His smile is contagious. "Thanks so much for coming on such short notice."

Okay, that sounded stiff and stupid. Like I should shake his hand.

"Hi, Avril. My pleasure." He leans in and kisses my cheek.

Okay, maybe the handshake would be overkill.

Mmm, nice eyes.

"I brought some help. This is Billy Ray Phillips. The two of us should be able to knock this out in no time."

"Hi, Billy Ray. Come in. Please." I step back to let them in.

"Pinch me," Lonnie Sue mutters from the kitchen door. "Did Christmas come early or am I dreamin' up this gorgeous vision of sugar plums standing here in this front room?"

The guys snicker.

Heat rises in my face. Mama, Gilda and Dani poke their heads from the kitchen. I want to kick Lonnie Sue, but that would only draw more attention.

"Let me introduce you to my mother, Tess Mulligan, and

to Gilda Mathers, Dani Reynolds and the infamous Lonnie Sue Tobias."

Shoulders back, chest out, Lonnie Sue dons her "man posture" and smiles coyly. "Thank you for coming, Max. I'm the one who called you. Avril's been so busy with things— and then Tess had a little accident and had to spend a night in the hospital—"

I clear my throat, a signal for Lonnie Sue to put a sock in it. "How about some dinner before we get started?"

They nod like polite men do when they want to say yes to food, but don't want to walk into a strange house and pile up a plate.

"I told y'all to come hungry," says Lonnie Sue. "So don't be shy. Come on in the kitchen. We have it all set out."

Billy Ray follows her as if she's the pied piper, but Max hangs back with me.

"Nice place," he says, glancing around the empty room.

I look around, too—at the freshly painted cream-colored walls, the fireplace on the east wall and the contrast of the white-painted baseboards with bare wooden floors—and try to see it through his eyes. Without any furniture, I suppose it's just another beach bungalow.

"Thanks." I shift from one foot to the other. He shoves his hand that's not holding his hat into his pocket. The gesture makes him seem a little nervous. That—and the fact that he brought a friend—softens me a little.

What kind of good-looking guy is available at a few hours' notice to help a virtual stranger mover her belongings? Especially when said virtual stranger ran out on him the last time he saw her and didn't even bother to call herself to ask for his help.

Persephone pipes up and says, *A nice guy. I mean, come on, he brought a friend. He can't be expecting the kind of payback Lonnie Sue was talking about—at least not tonight.*

"It's good to see you again," he says, looking me square in the eyes in that direct way of his that makes me feel a little off-kilter.

"Max, thanks for rounding up Billy Ray and coming out to help me tonight. I didn't know Lonnie Sue was calling you and to be honest, I'm a little embarrassed that she did."

His brow knits. "Now, why on earth would you be embarrassed? If it would've been inconvenient, I would've said no. It just so happens Billy Ray and I were looking for something to do tonight. So Lonnie Sue's call saved us from a night of pure boredom."

The way his brown eyes twinkle, I know he's pulling my leg. As if a man as good-looking as Max Wright would ever be reduced to searching for something to do. He probably had more women than he knew what to do with. So maybe we did happen to catch him on a slow night. Either that or he had to ditch someone to…move furniture.

Never mind.

I cross my arms over my pink T-shirt—the same one I'd had on since this morning—suddenly wishing I would've taken the time to change clothes.

When I glance up at him, he is studying my face. The way he's looking at me—almost appreciatively—makes my heart beat a little faster.

"Well, I just want you to know how much I appreciate your help."

He flashes a smile and a dimple winks at me from his right cheek. He takes a step closer and whispers, "Oh, I'll think of some way you can make it up to me."

His breath is minty clean, as if he just chewed a piece of gum, and his cologne is crisp with notes of green. Not as musky and heavy as Chet's— Umm…the one Chet *used* to wear.

I never really cared for it.

The thought smacks me, leveling any urge I might have had to breathe in deeper or move in closer.

Thinking of Chet causes the cycle of emotions to start again—grief, pain, Kally, disbelief, anger, grief…

"You know," he says, "I just thought of how you can pay me back, but we'll talk about it later because I'm sure dinner doesn't get any warmer than it is right now. Or does it?"

CHAPTER 15

The *payback* Max proposed wasn't what you're thinking. In fact, he was a perfect gentleman the entire night. He didn't even try to kiss me.

Of all things, he asked me to have dinner with him Saturday night.

Since the guy drove an hour each way to help me move, the least I can do is have dinner with him.

Even though I started the evening a woman who'd sworn off men, by the end of the night I had a date.

Anyhow, since I didn't bring much furniture with me, it didn't take very long to clear out the storage unit. Especially once we worked out a system: Max and Billy Ray did the hauling and heavy lifting. While they were gone, the girls and I unpacked boxes and put things away. Despite the gender-biased roles, it worked. In fact, I don't think I've ever had a move go so smoothly. Then again, the house is sparsely furnished. But that's okay. I kind of like this new minimalist way of life.

Less clutter.

Fewer things to weigh me down.

Except for my memories, which are taking up so much space they're spilling over into my dreams.

Last night I dreamt about Kally.

She and I were in that movie of Persephone that I worked on, but instead of me doing hair, *I* played the goddess Persephone to her Aphrodite.

I agreed to hide Adonis, who was actually Chet, but in the "movie" he was Aphrodite's lover. But when I saw how beautiful Adonis was, I fell head-over-heels for his charms and refused to give him back to Aphrodite.

Eventually, Zeus, who actually was my father—or at least the image I remember of my father from when he was still alive—stepped in and settled the argument. Then, you know how the lines and images in dreams tend to morph and change, well, suddenly we weren't Persephone and Aphrodite anymore. We were Kally and Avril and Chet, and my father ruled that Chet would spend a third of the year with me, a third of the year with Kally, and be left on his own the remainder of the year. But Chet chose to spend his free time with Kally and was looking for a way out of having to spend a third of the year with me.

Just like in the Greek myth.

When Kally and I were young, she had a crush on Chet. All the girls did, but she'd laid her claim on him first. Honoring one of the Friendship Commandments, the one that dictates *Thou shalt not covet they best friend's crush*, I worshiped him from afar. But when we were in the seventh grade and he finally decided he liked girls, he chose me.

Honoring the amendment to the Friendship Commandments that dictates *If the boy covets your best friend thou shalt step aside*, Kally stepped back and Chet and I…well, I suppose the rest is history.

And no, that commandment did not carry over to husbands coveting best friends after marriage. Don't be ridiculous.

Chet and I were together so long, it had been ages since I'd thought about how Kally liked him all those years ago. But in the wake of all that's happened, in light of this dream…it's all I've thought about today.

The dog barks.

I bend down and pet her. "It was just a dream. Thank God." But that doesn't alleviate the weight drawing my heart down to the pit of my stomach.

Talk to Kally, Persephone urges. *Or at least hear what she has to say.*

Instead, I talk to the dog.

"Hey, girl—you need a name. What should your name be?" Nothing fitting comes to mind and I have to go to work. So I decide to think about it, and decide, with a twinge of guilt, the best thing for both of us will be to keep her in the hall bathroom while I'm gone.

The yard is fenced, but I'm not sure if she's a digger or a barker and the last thing I need is to be the new neighbor with the nuisance dog.

"I'm sorry about this, but can you just eat your breakfast and hang in here until lunchtime? Then I'll come home and let you out?"

To entice her, I move her food.

Being relegated to the bathroom is no life for a dog. Especially one who's used to being footloose and fancy free. When I shut the door, she whines a little, but much to my relief, she doesn't go crazy barking.

It's nine o'clock by the time I walk to the salon. Mama has already opened the door but the shop is unusually quiet.

"Good morning," Mama calls. "I was just about to call you at home. I wasn't sure if you were coming in before ten since your first appointment isn't until then. But I just booked a nine-thirty haircut for you with Carolyn Heart."

I put my purse down at my station. "Good. Thank you." I walk over and pick up my appointment list. A pretty full day with a break in the middle for lunch.

"How was your first night at the new house?" Gilda asks as I set my purse down at my station.

"It was great. I slept like a rock."

Lonnie Sue listens with interest as she touches up her OPI nail color in her signature shade, *I'm Not Really a Waitress*, and Dani brings me a cup of coffee.

"Thanks so much," I say, accepting it gratefully. "I need to get myself a coffeemaker."

It strikes me how lucky I am that none of us holds grudges. I suppose that's why they've all worked with Mama for so many years.

The air is so copacetic it's hard to believe that at various times this week we were at each other's throats—sometimes literally—and now we're all gathered around talking like one big, happy family.

"Dani, I haven't had a chance to ask you before now, but how is everything with Tommy?" I ask.

Color blooms in her cheeks and she shrugs.

She picks up a brush and makes quick sweeps through her hair.

"How's Renie handling the separation?"

Dani's hand stops midstroke. "She's...*umm*... She's not taking it very well. But she knows things have been bad between her daddy and me for a long time."

Her voice cracks and I move to hug her, but she steps back and shakes her head. "I'm sorry, I just..."

"That's okay," I say.

"I wish I could've been strong and adventurous like you, Avril. I wish I would've gotten out of this town when I was young. And I would've never come—"

Eyes wide, she makes a little surprised gasp at what she almost said.

She would've never come back.

It stings, but I know she didn't mean it the way it sounded. I'm not going to turn this into ammunition for another fight.

I swallow hard and ignore the pang that this unintentional jab causes.

"Well, you know, Dani, it's never too late to spread your wings," I say.

Gilda sits down in the chair at her station and fixes her gaze on Dani. "That's right. With that girl of yours graduating in May, it'll be the perfect time to make a new start."

Dani opens her mouth to protest, but Gilda preempts as only Gilda can. "Now, I don't want to hear all the why-nots and I'm sure you've convinced yourself you have some pretty good, firm reasons. All I want you to do is think about it."

Dani nods and looks as if she's about to cry.

"Oh, come on, Gilda, get off the kid's case," says Mama. "She's working on coming to terms with this, and that's an awful lot."

The chime on the door sounds and we turn to see a woman standing in the threshold with the biggest, most beautiful arrangement of nearly every kind of flower you could imagine—red roses, sunflowers, irises, sweet peas…just to name a few—all arranged in a beautiful crystal vase.

"Is Avril Carson here?" she says.

My heart skips a beat. Honestly, my split-second thought when I saw the flowers was that they were for Lonnie Sue, then a wisp of hope that they were for Dani, an apology from Tommy, but that wouldn't have been good since he's no good for her and since flowers sometimes strike a soft spot in even the most levelheaded of women.

But they're for me. Oh…

Lonnie Sue squeals and points to me with the brush of her nail polish. "She's right there."

"Well, then, these are for you, hon. Could you sign here, please?"

Lonnie Sue wolf-whistles, and Mama, Gilda and Dani murmur—

"Would ya look at that?"

"How beautiful."

"What a romantic guy."

I thank the delivery woman, and before she leaves, she says, "Lucky girl. Someone sure likes you an awful lot."

"*Someone's* gonna get laid this weekend."

Mama frowns.

"Lonnie Sue, why do you always have to reduce everything to the bedroom?" Gilda chides.

"Who says it has to happen in the bedroom?" Lonnie Sue says. "That's so conventional, Gilda." She turns to me and in a stage whisper says, "Which translates to b-o-r-i-n-g."

Dani giggles and I bury my nose in the lovely arrangement, inhaling the sweet mélange of floral scent. I'm thirty-five years old, yet I'm still too embarrassed to look at my mother when someone mentions the word *sex*. It's not that I'm such a prude as much as it's just something my mother and I never talked about much beyond the good ol' birds and bees discussion, which I thought was going to cause her to have an aneurysm. My father died thirty years ago, and as far as I know, she's never even dated anyone, much less had sex—

The thought of her being alone all these years floors me. Surely, she's seen men. Maybe she just hasn't felt comfortable enough to tell me about them.

Persephone pipes up and says, *Did you ever ask?*

No!

Oh, grow up.

Maybe it's because I've never had children of my own and have remained in the daughter role, which is easy to do with a mother who mothers so well.

"What does the card say?" Dani asks.

I move a few things at my station to make room for the beautiful arrangement. As I'm opening the envelope, Mom's nine-fifteen appointment comes in—no one I know. She welcomes the woman, settles her in the chair and bustles around getting her coffee, but all the while I know she's listening to me read, "I'm counting the days until Saturday night."

Lonnie Sue lets out another hoot.

An odd heavy sort of feeling—a mixture of flattery and dread—washes over me.

"Oh, my," says Gilda.

"Wow," says Dani.

"Yep, someone's *definitely* getting laid. And Saturday night no less," says Lonnie Sue. "He's countin' the days."

Mama scowls. "Will y'all—" She draws her thumb and index finger across her lips. The international symbol for *Zip it*. With a slight nod of her head, she gestures discreetly toward her client, who is busy taking off her earrings. "*Please?*"

Lonnie Sue snorts and rolls her eyes, then takes my hand and pulls me into the back room. I'm still holding the card. I don't even have time to tuck it away somewhere private, where no one else will be able to read it before she abducts me. Dani follows, surely not wanting to miss anything.

"Well, look at you, hot stuff." Lonnie Sue gives me a good-natured tap on the arm. "Getting flowers from a gorgeous guy who's *counting the days until Saturday*. Oh, be still my heart." Her expression flashes from dreamy to scandalous. "Wait a minute. Did something happen last night after we left? Are you holding back?"

"No! Nothing happened. Billy Ray was there. How could anything happen? I mean *not* that anything would've happened if Billy Ray hadn't been there—"

"And why not?" demands Lonnie Sue.

"Yeah," echoes Dani. "Why not?"

I close my hand around the card as if by covering it I can

will it to disappear. But the edges bite into my palm, making it clear that it's not going anywhere.

"Well…because."

Two blank faces stare back at me, confused. Like I'm speaking a foreign language they don't understand.

"Well, what about Saturday night?" She crosses her arms over her ample chest and perches her butt on the edge of the small table, settling in for the full story.

I shrug. "What about it?"

"Oh, you are impossible!" they both say at once or at least variations of the accusation.

"Where is he taking you Saturday night, and by this I'm assuming that you *did* say yes when he asked you out."

I shrug again, almost enjoying the game.

"Oh, come on!" says Dani. "He's gorgeous and tall and drops everything to move furniture at a moment's notice and then sends *you* flowers for the privilege of doing it. Please tell us you *did* say yes."

I give them my poker face for a few more seconds, but then I can't keep a smile from breaking through.

"Yes, we're going out Saturday night."

Going out. The words hang in the air and sound weird to my ears. So I chase them away with, "He's taking me out to dinner."

"That's Valentine's Day," Lonnie Sue informs me.

Valentine's Day?

They both squeal and start talking at once—

"What are you going to wear?"

"Do you want me to do your hair?"

"Are you nervous? Excited? Completely and totally in *love*?"

"Are you going to sleep with him?" Lonnie Sue's voice rings triumphant over Dani's and her words linger, palpable, as if she painted the question on the wall in bold letters with a bright red heart around it.

I shake my head. "*No*, I'm not going to sleep with him."

"And why not?" Lonnie Sue demands. "It's *Valentines Day*."

"I missed the memo announcing cheap sex as the new Valentine."

"Who says it has to be cheap? Unless you want to go on a sliding scale as to how much he shells out for dinner." She laughs at her own joke.

Surely she's joking.

"You're sick," I say. "It's going to be a long time before I wind up in a man's bed."

"Well, what about *your* bed?" Lonnie Sue says. "Kissimmee's more than an hour away. Surely you're not going to make him drive home after the dance, are you? What if ya'll have wine?"

"Or champagne," Dani says.

Oh. I hadn't even thought about that. Would he expect to stay? Is that how it is now? After a lifetime of being with one man—did I mention that Chet is the only man I've ever slept with?

Oh, I'm so out of my league here.

I'm not good at this dating thing. Since I knew Chet practically all my life, I always felt comfortable around him. We just sort of grew into each other, grew up with each other and into each new stage of romance. There was never this awkwardness.

Maybe awkwardness means it's all wrong?

"This is our first date…." I say.

"No, it's not," says Lonnie Sue. "He took you to coffee and then he helped you move—" She holds up two fingers. "Technically, this'll be date number three and you know what that means!"

"This is *not* our third date!"

"Well, let me ask you this," Dani cuts in. "Why *wouldn't* you sleep with him? You like him, don't you?"

I'm not believing this. "I *barely know* him?"

"Well, you know you like him. You know he's a decent guy. And a damn good-lookin' one at that." Lonnie Sue's eyes shine with possibility.

We're all silent for a moment. I'm trying to process everything. Trying to find a way out of this dead-end conversation and if that doesn't work, trying to figure out how to explain that just twenty-four hours ago I was opposed to the idea of even seeing him again, much less having sex with the guy.

"You know," Dani says in a small voice, "if I were you— and let's face it, our situations are a little similar…."

No, our situations are vastly different. Her cheating husband is alive. At least she can hate him—guilt free—for what he's done. Mine is dead. How can you hate a dead man? Isn't that sacrilegious?

"If I were you," she continues, "I'd sleep with Max for vindication or better yet as a sort of emancipation."

I'm so stunned by this thought I can't even speak. Everything from *What a terrible thing to do to Max* to *Why not?* whirls through my mind in a split second. But I can't linger on that last thought very long because if the truth be told, I'm not *there* yet. You know, I can't imagine sharing that intimate part of myself with another man. I wish I could simply divorce my emotions from the action, as if I were divorcing Chet, and just go in there and have a hell of a night with a gorgeous man and call the score even.

But knowing myself like I do, I'd really just be hurting myself in the end. I can't even imagine how it would affect Max. *If* it would affect him. And it would be almost worse if it *didn't*.

Or would it?

Okay, do you see, how *not* ready for this I am? These are the facets of a relationship I'm not ready to deal with.

"So is that what you're going to do to get back at Tommy? Go out and sleep with someone to even the playing field?"

Dani shakes her head, looking a little sheepish. "I started

to tell you earlier…Tommy and I are…talking. We're trying to work things out."

"What? Really? Why?" Gilda's voice drifts in the open door and melds with mine and Lonnie Sue's shouts of surprise. She appears in the doorway with her hands on her hips, a feather duster tightly clinched in her fist and an incredulous look on her face. "Aren't you concerned about sending a bad message to your daughter?"

"He's my husband," Dani says. "I can't just give up on him. He says he's sorry. Say's he'll change."

"Have you ever heard of the saying *fool me once, shame on you—fool me twice shame on me?*" Gilda says.

Dani doesn't answer her. She stares at the fingernails on her left hand and picks at the chipped polish on her ring finger.

Gilda turns her gaze on me. "And as for you, missy, everything I've heard says sleeping with a guy too soon is a relationship killer."

I flinch because I had no idea she was listening to what we were talking about.

Embarrassment, white-hot and heavy, blooms on my cheeks. I wonder if Mama heard us? But a quick glance out the door proves her busy chatting to her client, obliviously combing and sectioning off pieces of damp hair, trimming off the uneven ends and repeating the process over again.

"Dani, you and me are gonna chat later," says Lonnie Sue. "In the meantime, Gilda, honey, you are too old-fashioned for your own good. Hell, if I like a guy, I make a point of sleeping with him on the *first* date."

"Yeah, and look at where it's gotten you," Gilda challenges.

Lonnie Sue rolls her eyes. "I guess I'm just not the type who plays games. I mean, what's the use of being coy when you know it's what you both want?" She puts her hands on her hips and climbs up on her virtual soapbox. "Even more, why is it okay for guys to have sex right out of the gate but if the woman does she's a slut?"

Gilda pretends to be disgusted as she always does when Lonnie Sue pulls a good argument out of her hat and Gilda is stumped for a valid retort.

"Hey, guys, I don't even know if I want to keep seeing him. So let's not get ahead of ourselves."

"Well, if you don't want to see him," says Dani, who has taken a cotton of nail polish remover to her damaged manicure, "and if what Gilda says about fast sex being a relationship killer is true, maybe you should just go out and have yourself a real good time. Take back your power—show that what was good for Chet is good for you, too."

Oh.

Her words slam into me like a fist. The bald, hard truth of Chet's betrayal hurts and suddenly I'm not sure if I can even go through with the date.

MY DAD DIED WHEN I was five. After that, it was just my mother and me. She never dated or found anyone else. I wonder if it was in tribute to my father or if she did look and never found anyone.

I used to have this romantic notion that there's one perfect someone out there for each person. Maybe I've seen one too many Hollywood romances where destiny kicks in and despite bad hair, different social classes and force majeure, love triumphs over all; two perfect souls who are destined for each other overcome seemingly insurmountable odds and live happily ever after.

If only that's the way it really works.

Whatever the case, my dad seemed to be the one and only love of my mother's life.

I have this vague memory of my father coming home from work and lifting me in the air and swinging me around. Everything was a blur, except for his handsome face, which is forever imprinted on my mind. Or maybe it's a memory I've manufactured after years of pouring over old photographs.

If you get Mama started talking about him, she always gets all misty-eyed and sentimental as if she lost him yesterday. That's what happens after I finish with my last morning appointment and Mama asks me to go across the street to the Sago Diner to grab a quick bite of lunch.

From the start, I can tell she has something on her mind,

and I have a very strong hunch that it has something to do with the girls drilling me about the first-date sex dilemma.

But just in case I was wrong, I wasn't about to be the first to bring it up. So we make small talk about the house, the dog, the different selections on the lunch menu, whether we should be good or splurge on a treat. She finally settles on the patty melt and I order a chef salad.

After we have our drinks, she asks, "Are you having a salad because of your date on Saturday?"

I run my finger along a crack in the Formica tabletop. "Is this your subtle way of telling me I need to shed a few pounds?"

Ignoring my sarcasm, she props her elbow on the table and brings her fingers together, steepling them in front of her face like a sanctuary she can hide behind.

"So he asked you to dinner?"

I nod again, realizing she must have heard every word of what we were saying. Either that or Gilda relayed the conversation, which would've been a verbatim retelling, I'm sure. But we were so busy this morning, I don't know Gilda would've had time.

"That's a long drive home for him."

She pauses, sips her sweet tea. I have a sneaking suspicion of what she's dancing around.

"Will he stay over?"

"Mama."

She stares somewhere over my shoulder. Shrugs. "I'm

just saying you're a grown woman. And you're still a young woman. I hope that you won't let this whole ordeal keep you from finding someone else."

I start to protest, to resurrect every argument I presented in the back room of the salon, but she silences me with a single movement of her hand—just like she's always been able to do.

"He seems to be a nice guy, Avril. I'm not saying you should start looking for a wedding dress. I'm just saying give him a chance."

An awkward silence envelops us. It's strange because I've never felt uncomfortable with my mother. She's always been my touchstone. The one true person I can be myself with, not have to pretend. In the end I was pretending with Chet— pretending like I could live Hollywood-style. For him.

"Maybe it would help if you sprinkled his ashes, honey? It would give you some closure."

Sometimes it kind of freaks me out how it seems like she can read my mind. Oh, the ashes…yes…

It's been a year since he died. I wanted to bring him home. I couldn't bring myself to scatter his ashes in California. It felt like leaving him there.

Persephone pipes up, *Maybe that would've been the best thing, seeing how much he changed. How in the end he became a person you didn't even recognize.*

I blink away the thought.

But shouldn't I wait until I'm at a better place with him? Until I've sorted out what he did, how he lied? Until I can get some peace?

It's too much for me to process right now. So I change the subject. "Mama, why didn't you ever date after daddy died?"

Ironic tenderness slips over her face. I recognize this look. She's falling backward through the tunnel of years, floating in memories of long ago.

"He was a special man, honey. He sure was." She shakes her head wistfully, keeping her gaze downcast. "Nobody better. Not to this very day."

A faraway smile slips across her face, and I try to imagine what it must be like to have loved the memory of one man for all these years. Thirty years from now, I don't know if I'll be able to do it. To remember the good. Too many things had happened, too many things that were supposed to be rock solid have turned to sand and scattered on the storm of deceit and adultery.

"Do you miss him?"

She sighs. "Oh, yes. Of course I do." She fidgets with her silverware and then picks imaginary lint off her sleeve. When she looks at me her eyes are liquid. "It was thirty years this past May. And the hurt is there like it was yesterday."

I reach out and touch her hand.

She looks up at me with those misty eyes, a little startled, as if she forgot I was actually sitting across from her.

"I don't mean it's never going to get better for you, baby. It will. I have my good days and better days. But that's just how it is."

She manages a smile and sits back in the seat, straight and tall, like she's physically put away the sadness. "So, let's not end up being two old widows, okay? You keep yourself open to finding another man, okay?"

I know I shouldn't push it, but I do. "You never answered my question. Why didn't you find someone else?"

She's silent for a moment. I can see her thinking as she traces the rim of her red plastic tea glass.

Finally she says, "I had you. That and the memory of your daddy was plenty enough for me."

"I guess when you have kids, it sort of changes the dynamics. Well, that's nothing I'll have to worry about."

In my mind's eye, I see Kally and Sam as they looked in that photo on her desk. Before the leukemia took its toll and stole her beauty. In my mind, I try to superimpose Chet into that photo, but even though I know what he looks like, I can't form a mental picture of him. Is he already fading?

Maybe it's that I can't form a picture of *them*. Together.

One small, happy family.

"When was the last time you saw Kally?" I ask.

Mama flinches at the non sequitur. "I have no idea."

She spits the words as if they've left a bad taste in her mouth.

"Did you know she's sick?"

She shakes her head and shrugs, like it's the least of her problems.

"No, Mama, I'm serious. She's really sick. She has leukemia."

Her hand flutters to her neck.

"Oh, my dear God in heaven. Are you serious?"

I nod. "She looks terrible. I'm surprised no one around here's seen her and said anything. For that matter, I'm surprised Gilda didn't tell you how bad she looked after she saw her at the hospital the other night."

"She was at the hospital?"

"Yes, she drove Lonnie Sue and me. Didn't they tell you? Juicy gossip like that?"

She arches her brows and leans in as if she's telling a secret. "With all the trouble their gossiping's caused, they're lying kind of low on that front with me."

"Oh, I see."

We're quiet for a minute, but the thought of Kally looms between us as if she's here.

"Who's looking after her and that boy of hers?"

"I don't know. She seems to have a good relationship with this one guy who works for her. He seems pretty protective of her, but he's just a kid. I can't imagine that he'd be there if she got really sick…. I mean—"

Then like a flash flood I can't stop the tears. They come

from out of nowhere, pouring from my eyes, racking me with great sobs that shake my body.

I can't stop crying.

Mama reaches across the table and squeezes my arm, grabs a wad of napkins with the other and gives them to me.

"I know, baby, I know. I'm so, so, sorry."

I bury my face in my hands and sob until I've cried myself out, not caring who sees me or what they might say.

When I finally raise my tearstained face, our lunches are waiting for us. I have no idea how long they've been there or who stealthily slipped in the delivery.

It doesn't really matter.

Because I don't know that anyone in this town would understand how I could cry for a woman who betrayed me in the worst possible way a friend could betray a friend; a friend who, for so many years, meant so much to me I could almost feel her pain as if what plagued her was happening to me.

Perhaps that's what I'm feeling right now.

As if reading my mind, Mama says, "You want to go to her, don't you?"

CHAPTER 16

My last appointment leaves just before three-thirty. Since my lunch-hour breakdown I've vacillated between contacting Kally and not; I thought about calling her, which I determined would be pointless, finally deciding to go see her because it would be better to hear her out in person.

I'll just pop in.

Throw it up to fate.

If she's there, so be it.

If she's not—well, I tried.

Mama offers me her car, which is the straw that tips me in favor of going. I didn't ask. I was ready to *think about* it a little more, when she pulls me aside and whispers, "Why don't you take my car and go see Kally?"

When I hesitate, she says in a low, tender voice, "Honey, I know this is hard and I know you've barely had time to let it all sink in, but y'all have been friends for so long and she's sick. You take my car and go see her—don't let this wait."

I glance at the girls to see if their ears have perked up

since Mama and I have put our heads together. But they're all busy. I'm glad because I'm not ready to let them in on this. Not yet. And I suppose not until I have a chance to talk to Kally…

And what flashes through my mind is a mix of thoughts ranging from I'm-perfectly-justified-to-never-talk-to-Kally-again petty to death-waits-for-no-one profound.

Because what Mama is really trying to say to me is, *You don't have time to let this go.*

In light of everything that happened—my daddy, Chet—you'd think I might have learned this lesson.

As I'm climbing into Mama's cherry-red T-Bird feeling sick to my stomach, I toss it up to fate. If Kally's there, I'm supposed to do this. If she's not…

Okay, we'll cross that bridge if we come to it.

I PARALLEL PARK on the street in front of Lady Marmalade's and sit there for a minute with the window rolled down, inhaling the humid, sea air. The smell of my youth, the scent of my home—a place where I still belong even if I feel slightly displaced. L.A. smelled different. I can't exactly put my finger on the subtle difference, but it did. There was a note of desperation floating in the air and I always seemed to be downwind of it; the pressure to be better, prettier, thinner—more than you were or could ever be. That's the only song your subconscious could sing—the ballad of *No Matter What You Do, You'll Never Be Quite Good Enough*.

What a sad, sad song to get stuck in your head.

In the distance, I hear the faint roar of the tide and the random squawk of gulls, all overshadowed by the sound of light traffic.

Several people come and go through the purple-and-chartreuse-painted front door of Lady Marmalade's Coffeehouse.

Leukemia.

Chet. Kally slept with Chet.

How can you turn your back on her at a time like this?

"Stop it!"

I open the car door with such force that it bounces back and hits my knee.

Just calm down.

I try again. This time I am deliberate in my movements, pushing the door open, planting my feet on the pavement and putting one Prada-clad foot in front of the other until I reach the door.

At least today I'm clean and I'm wearing shoes. That thought propels me through the open door. Good thing, because there's no turning back now.

Lady Marmalade's is just as busy today as it was the last time I was here. But after a cursory glance around the place, I don't see Kally. Just Surfer Boy, the girl who was working with him the other day and another guy I don't recognize.

Normally, the smell of good coffee would comfort me, entice me to slow down and have a cup. But I wonder, as I stand there, if I'll ever be able to smell it again without getting a knot in the pit of my stomach.

I want to turn around and leave.

Go ask if she's here, prods Persephone.

I can't. I really don't think I can do this.

Yes. You. Can.

Standing there in the doorway of the artsy coffeehouse, I have the surreal sensation of being stuck in one of those dreams where you're desperately trying to make your limbs work, but no matter how hard you try, you can't.

Surfer Boy glances over and offers a hearty, "Welcome to Lady Marmalade's." But he's back to helping customers before he figures out it's me. Given my respectable appearance today, he probably has no idea who I am.

Someone opens the door behind me, forcing me to move out of the way. Next thing I know, as if I'm propelled by an unseen force, I find myself at the counter, facing Surfer Boy, "Is Kally in?"

The flicker of recognition registers in his eyes. The wall goes up. "Nope. She's not here right now. But I'll tell her you came by."

His stare pierces me. Like he's afraid if he takes his gaze off me, I'll turn into the crazed Creature from the Black Lagoon who invaded Lady Marmalade's a few days ago.

"Thank you," I say.

I tried. She wasn't here. I tossed it up to fate and got my answer.

Fighting tears, I make my way to the exit. As I reach for the knob, the door swings open and—

Oh—

Kally stands there holding the hand of a little boy.

Sam.

Kally gasps. "Avril!" She says my name as if I'm the very person she's wished to see before twisting the knob of a magic door.

"Hi. I was just…"

My voice breaks and honestly, I don't know what *I was just… I was just* wanting to talk to you…. *I was just* leaving….

I was just so damn sick that everything had to turn out the way it has.

But now that she's here, by the agreement I made with the universe, I suppose that means I have to stay and do what I have to do. Cursed fate, playing the old bait and switch on me.

"Please don't leave," she says. She's so earnest it catches me off guard. I don't say anything because I don't know what to say, and I guess she takes that as a sign that I'm staying.

She reaches out with a bony hand. Her fingers flutter in the air, but she stops short of touching me, as if she knows better. "*Please* come in."

Her hands fall to the shoulders of the boy. "Avril, this is Sam."

She pauses a moment, staring down at him with pride.

"Sam, this is Avril Carson, a very special person to me. Come on, Avril, let me get you some coffee. What would you like? A latte? A mocha? Cappuccino?"

I look at the boy, who stares up at me in that unabashed way of little kids. He looks so much like Chet, it takes my breath away. Same direct, bright blue gaze, same cleft chin, same way of furrowing his brow.

Oh, my—

"I'm sorry, I can't stay."

Only Kally and Sam are blocking the door.

My heart pounds and for a terrible moment, I want to push past them, but that one last sensible vein in me that didn't perish in the wreck that my life has become won't allow me to do that.

"No, really, I can't stay. I just stopped by to see if you could come by tonight. Umm, you said you wanted to talk— er, to tell me something. And tonight's good."

THE DOORBELL RINGS AT SEVEN.

The dog goes crazy barking and I drop the lid to the pasta pot, managing to burn myself in the process. Kally always was prompt. Obviously she hasn't changed in that way.

When I finally get myself together and answer the

door, she's standing there with a bottle of wine and a small package.

The dog runs in circles around her and then jumps up, scratching at her jeans.

"Get down." I pull her away.

"Oh, she's so cute." Kally bends down and scratches her behind the ears. The traitor flops down and rolls over on her back giving Kally ample access to her belly.

"You're so cute." Kally squats down and talks baby talk to the dog. "What's your name?"

Benedictine Arnold. No, Judas. Either one would suit, you ungrateful animal. Thanks for being on my side.

"She doesn't have a name yet. I just found her a couple of days ago."

The dog wiggles to her feet and puts her paws on Kally's shoulders so she can lick her face.

Kally laughs, but doesn't push her away. "Oh, Sam would love you. He wants a doggy so bad."

"Maybe they can meet someti—" *Oh, my God. Did I just say that? I can't believe I said that. Wait! Rewind. I didn't mean it.*

"Yes!" Kally looks up at me and her blue eyes shine.

She tweaks the dog's ear, gathers the wine and package, then pushes to her feet. "That would make him *so* happy."

Feeling a little betrayed by myself and the dog, I consider telling her to take the unfaithful animal home. But then I'm afraid she'll take me up on it so I say nothing.

"Here." She holds out the goods. "A housewarming present."

I take them, avoiding her gaze. She steps into the living room and looks around.

"Where is Sam?" I ask.

"Zane's watching him."

Surfer Boy?

"Is he your boyfriend?"

What is wrong with me? It's like I've developed a sudden case of Tourette's syndrome. Her love life is none of my concern, and honestly, I really don't care.

"Zane?" Kally wrinkles her nose, as if she's never considered him in that light. "Oh, no. He's just a good friend. He's a sweet kid."

She laughs that familiar laugh that used to always make me smile. Our history flashes through my mind—the sleepovers, the secrets, the hopes and dreams and fights and make-ups. All that time she and Jake Brumly, Chet and I— the fearsome foursome—spent together. I wonder where Jake is now, but I don't ask.

It's such a dichotomy, the sound of her laugh. It both warms and saddens me.

But as I stand there staring at this person who is so familiar, yet at the same time is such a stranger—like an actress who is playing a role I'm unfamiliar with—I decide it's just that kind of night.

One big dichotomy.

I open the package—a beautiful, fat red candle sitting in a gold star holder.

"I remember how you used to always like candles." She crosses her arms—a protective shield.

"Remember how we used to stay up until the wee hours of the morning talking? We couldn't go to sleep until the candle burned itself out. We used to say it was bad luck. Remember?"

All I can do is nod.

She follows me into the kitchen, watches me place the candle in the center of the table. We stand there, facing the mountain between us. Neither of us knowing where to start or if we'll ever reach the other side.

Dinner is awkward.

Like most enamored mothers, Kally talks incessantly about Sam. Her hollow-jawed face lights up when she speaks of him—how smart he is, how he can count to one hundred and recognize most basic words. How he wants to learn to read before he gets to kindergarten.

He knows she's sick, but not the details—he's only four, for heaven's sake. But he loves to take care of her.

The candle she brought is lit, but all I can do is listen, feeling somewhat detached. We covered the *when* and *why* of her and Chet at Lady Marmelade's that day.

I really can't think of anything else to talk about.

She and I have nothing in common anymore now; she's a mother and I can't have kids. She's slept with my husband and I hate women who do that.

There's barely a dent in this candle.

What on earth did we used to talk about all those years ago as the wax burned down? It seemed like we could never get enough. If we weren't together, we were talking on the phone?

When did it all slip away? I know California was a long way from Sago Beach, but weren't friends supposed to be able to pick up where they left off?

In the light of what's happened, it feels like this is the end of the line. Except for—

"Did Chet come for the birth?"

She looks as confused as I feel about the question, as if I've asked it in Japanese.

"He traveled a lot," I say. "I've tried to remember where he was around that time, but that was more than four years ago."

"No, he didn't come back." She pushes her half-full plate away and doesn't look at me as she answers.

"So you were on your own when Sam was born?"

She shrugs. "You do what you have to do."

I take my napkin out of my lap, fold it and place it to the side of my place setting, suddenly tired and impatient.

"Kally, why are you here? What did you want to talk to me about?"

She stares at the table for a moment, smooths the tablecloth, then folds her hands.

"I want you to know how sorry I am this happened."

"You've already told me." The words sound like angry sniper fire.

"I never meant to hurt you. *You* of all people, Av. You're my family and other than Sam the *only* family I have left."

We're quiet for a moment and I wonder if she expects me to say something. Because I can't. Sitting here, looking at her earnest face, listening to her apology, I'm absolutely numb. Because if I let myself feel, it would be anger that burned through.

I wonder if this feeling will plague me the rest of my life. Is that how people become hardened and bitter?

"Do you remember how we used talk about being godmothers to each other's children?" she says.

I stare at her, with a sick feeling that I know where she's going, not believing she'd have the audacity to ask what I think she's going to ask.

"Yes, but that was before…"

I want to say *that was before you became someone I don't recognize. Even if you did apologize, it doesn't change what you did.*

I'm dying to say it. I have to bite my tongue to keep from spitting the words at her. The only reason I don't let her have it is because before she got here I promised myself this wouldn't turn ugly. This wouldn't digress into a name-calling, insult-slinging verbal slugfest.

"That was before *this*," I say.

"I know and I know I have no right to ask…."

Did she not hear me?

She dabs at her eyes.

"Av, I don't know how much longer I have left. The doctor's prognosis was not good. I mean, I want to kick it. I'm doing everything I can, but the reality is—"

Her voice catches.

I want to tell her to stop. I want to scream *How dare you?* How dare you both betray me and then die?

"Avril, if anything happens to me, I want you to adopt Sam." She reaches out and takes my hand. "Sam doesn't have anyone else. My mom's gone, Chet's parents are dead. Please?"

I blow out the candle.

"I think you should leave."

CHAPTER 17

The Saturday after my dinner with Kally—on Valentine's Day, the day I'm supposed to go out with Max—it finally dawns on me what's different about her: audacity.

She never had such nerve all the years I've known her. She used to be quiet and amiable—never one to rock the boat. She's changed more than I realized. Never in a million years would I have thought her capable of doing something so out of character as sleeping with my husband and then having the *audacity* to ask me to be the godmother of their love child.

It's really kind of mind-blowing.

I pointedly ignore the twinge of guilt that stabs at me.

She has leukemia. How can you be so angry?

The dog, who still doesn't have a name, looks up at me. "I'm sorry. I can't help it. Don't you think I deserve a little slack here?"

She puts her head on her paws and stares up at me with worried brown eyes.

"I know Kally has had a hard life losing her mother and now this leukemia…."

For obvious reasons, I don't add *and she's raising a kid on her own*. That certainly doesn't entitle her to…to…to put me on the spot, expecting me to forgive and forget and adopt her kid.

"Chet's kid."

The dog cocks her head to the right in that way of hers.

Persephone pipes up, *If Chet were alive, that's what you'd do. You'd adopt the kid.*

"Oh, no. If Chet were alive, he'd be raising this boy on his own."

Would he? Would you really walk out on him over this? Break that "til death do us part' vow?

"He's the one who blew it wide open when he slept with Kally. So don't even start playing the broken vow card with me."

Oh, and what was it you said to Kally the other day about two wrongs not making a right? You being mean and nasty to her in her time of need.

"Oh, go away, Miss *Thang*."

The dog barks.

"What? Either you think I'm crazy talking to myself or you think I'm talking to you, Miss *Thang*."

Bark. Bark-bark.

"You like that name? Miss *Thang*."

The little animal runs in circles barking, then rears up on her back legs and braces her front paws on me, licking my hand when I reach down to pet her.

"So I guess you have a name."

AFTER MY LAST CLIENT leaves at four o'clock, the salon is empty of clients. Mama's gone down to the bank to make the daily deposit. In preparation for the big date tonight, Gilda is doing my hair; she washes it for me and blows it straight with a large round brush. My hair is a little wavy—especially in this humidity. It doesn't take much to straighten it out, but it never looks the same when I try to do it myself—no matter how many years I've been working magic on other people's hair. Besides, it's relaxing. To me there's nothing quite so soothing as someone else doing my hair.

Actually, I'm getting the royal treatment. Lonnie Sue, who received three huge bouquets of flowers today—none of which were from Sheriff Sid Olsen, which made her all the more determined to "win" him—is giving me a pedicure. Dani, who has been rather quiet on this romantic day, is painting my nails.

I appreciate this pampering. It takes my mind off the predate butterflies that have been flying in formation since after lunch.

As soon as Gilda turns off the blow dryer and reaches for the glossing serum, Dani announces, "I have some good news. Tommy and I have worked things out. He's moving back in."

Lonnie Sue and Gilda dart quick glances at each other and then at me. I can hear us thinking in unison—this is the same old pattern.

Dani puts the cap back on the polish and reaches for the quick-dry topcoat.

"He promises to quit drinking." She sounds defensive as she applies the polish in quick swipes. Her tone is urgent, trying to convince us that *this time* he's really changed.

"How in the world can you sit here and tell us this?" Lonnie Sue pushes to her feet, the shock obviously giving way to anger. "I mean what do you expect us to do? Honey, we want to be supportive, but how can you expect us to watch you go back to a man who has treated you like shit and left marks to prove it?"

"Do you have no self-respect?" Gilda looks truly flummoxed.

Dani stares at my fingers as she applies the last stroke of topcoat. Her throat works as she swallows.

She's quiet until she screws the cap back on and puts the bottle back on the tray.

"Tommy is my husband. I owe it to myself to do everything in my power to make this work. I can't just toss in the towel after eighteen years of marriage."

I READ SOMEWHERE that one reason men cheat is because of a biological urge to propagate. Not literally. They don't screw around with the express purpose of populating the planet. This report said men are hardwired to procreate and that gives them the urge to sniff around the henhouse next door.

Sounds like a load of bull to me.

Of course, the article went on to say that although men

may be predisposed to cheat, it's not something they can't overcome.

As I put the finishing touches on my makeup—Max should be here to pick me up in fifteen minutes or so—I wonder if somehow Dani read this same article and that's why she's so willing to forgive Tommy his transgressions?

Actually, what I'm wondering is whether she's a saint or a fool. Could I have been so forgiving of Chet if he were still alive?

Perhaps the better question is will I be able to forgive him now that he's dead. Really, the only difference is that I won't have to look at him every day and wonder—does he love her or me? Will he cheat with someone else? Was I not woman enough to keep my husband satisfied in his own bed?

Blush brush poised midair, I study myself in the bright light of the vanity table mirror—the low-cut black blouse I've paired with jeans, wanting to be casual and sexy. Desirable. Only now, I feel as if I should go put on something more respectable and take the condoms I bought out of my purse. Good girls don't show so much cleavage.

And they don't carry rubbers in their handbags.

Unless they intend to get laid.

"What am I doing?"

An ache starts in my chest and migrates south to that barren spot in my belly where a child should've grown.

I drop the brush and cover my tummy with my hands. But that doesn't stop the pain from nearly paralyzing me.

I don't want to see Max tonight.

It's Valentine's Day, and I just can't do it.

I'm not ready for this.

What if he brings flowers and a cheesy heart-shaped box of chocolate? What if he expects romance on this most romantic night of the year?

I've been psyching myself up for an emotionally detached roll in the hay—just like Dani and Lonnie Sue said.

Why not have a little fun? Take back my power?

Good old hot no-strings-attached sex on the first date. That's sure to get rid of him—and maybe even put a skip in my step.

But with each second the clock ticks closer to time for Max to pick me up, a little piece of my bravado falls away, until all that remains is a false front even skimpier than this blouse I bought especially for tonight.

I tug the neckline up, trying to cover my exposed cleavage. But there's not enough shirt.

I can't go through with it. Who am I kidding, thinking I can separate sex and emotion? I'm not Lonnie Sue.

There's just been too much loss in my life, too many failures. In fact, right now, it seems like my life's been one long chain of loss and failure: my failed dream of being a star, my unsatisfying life in California, my husband and father who both died much too young, my best friend who betrayed me and the baby I'll never have….

I could call Max and cancel. Tell him that I'm sick—which wouldn't exactly be a lie—

All right, look, quips Persephone. I can almost see her in the mirror smirking at me over my shoulder, all exasperation and disgust. *Snap out of it, babe, and play the hand you were dealt. If you're ever going to work your way out of this mire, you can't wallow. Ya wallow, ya sink. You may be starting over from the bottom, but at least you have a direction to go.*

And tonight that direction is straight out the front door on a date with a gorgeous man.

You don't have to sleep with him.

Unless you want to.

Feeling as if I'm coming up from underwater, I shake my head, then sit there until I finally convince myself she's right.

Plus, he'll be here any minute. I can't back out now.

But tonight will be on my terms.

I never have to see him again after this if I don't want to.

And if he brings me candy, I give myself permission to call it an early evening, come home alone and have my own private chocolate orgy.

RUSTY'S BAIT AND RAW BAR is a legend in these parts. Located about twenty miles south of Sago Beach, it's an open-walled, tin-roofed shack on stilts sitting over the water. From land, it looks like a giant, long-legged bird perched at the end of the rickety dock that stretches into the Cypress River.

It's been here as far back as I can remember and was a big part of my teenage years. As we turn into the crowded parking lot, bittersweet nostalgia hits me head-on.

Rusty's party-worn edges have aged into a patina that hints the place has been here as long as the dunes have lined the beach.

Growing up in these parts, I know the difference between "aged" and dirty. So do most locals, who come here for the fresh catch and a fun place to party. Joints like this earn their keep by offering good fresh fish, cold beer and loud live music out on the open deck. If it were *dirty* or served anything but the best seafood, it wouldn't be as packed as it is on this warm Saturday night.

As Max parks his truck in front of a tall, skinny-trunked palm tree at the far side of the crowded parking lot, a sense of relief washes over me: *he brought me here instead of trying to wine and dine me at some fancy restaurant.*

And by the way, no roses and cheesy heart-shaped box of chocolate. Just a single blood-red Gerber daisy, which earns him points for originality.

The bar is far enough away from home that the likelihood of running into someone I know is very small.

Suddenly, the night's beginning to look up.

Max walks around and opens my door. He left his hat at home tonight—probably a good idea—and traded in his usual uniform of head-to-toe black for a cobalt-blue button-down, a pair of Levi's and boots. The minute I step out of the truck I hear the music. I breathe in the scent of kerosene mingling with the marsh and what smells like beer and shrimp boil.

While we walk the length of the dock strung with tiny white lights and flaming tiki torches, a gentle breeze silvers the water that's flushed pink by the waning sun. The river lies between the open-air deck and a dense stand of palmettos about one hundred feet away. Sunburned people dance and cluster around newspaper-covered tables, drinking beer from bottles and eating oysters and peel-it-yourself shrimp.

At the far end of the deck, a Jimmy Buffett wanna-be sits on a stool, strumming an acoustic guitar and singing "Cheeseburger in Paradise" into a microphone on a stand.

Revelers laugh and talk and occasionally shout out lines of the song—like the part about liking a burger with *lettuce and tomato…Heinz 57 and French-fried potatoes…* The party has obviously been going on for a long time.

But the music and the unpretentious beachy ambiance take me back to a simpler time.

And it makes me smile.

"This way." Max grabs my hand and navigates the throngs of people. My hand feels small in his and there's something about the unselfconscious way he links his finger through mine that sets me at ease.

We stop near the rail, a few feet away from the singer.

"So you've been here before?" I say.

"Yep. My family and I used to spend the summers over here and my brother and I used to walk to this place—for the food, of course."

Chet hated Rusty's. I teased him that he couldn't stomach the words *Bait* and *Raw Bar* in the same restaurant name— especially when Bait came first. So Kally and I would steal away here for a girls' night out whenever her mother would let her take the car. We were only sixteen, frightfully underage, but back then, it didn't seem to matter. And Rusty's was far enough away that we rarely saw anyone who would tell on us.

"God, I haven't been here in ages." The memory of the night Kally wrecked the car nudges at the edges of my memory, but I mentally swat it away like a gnat that's buzzing in my space.

"Really? You used to hang out here?" he asks.

The singer shifts into "Margaritaville," and I watch a couple try to slow dance to the song.

"Another lifetime ago."

"Ahh, before those mysterious, lost California years," Max says. "How long were you there?"

NANCY ROBARDS THOMPSON   203

"A long, long time." I don't want to get in to it.

The people at the table next to us motion us over as they stand to leave. Prime real estate—overlooking the water, right up against the deck railing.

"Are you always this lucky?" I ask as Max pulls out a chair for me.

He leans in and whispers in my ear, "I guess that remains to be seen." Then he winks at me and my stomach turns upside down at the innuendo, which is strange, because under normal circumstances I'd find it off-putting.

Maybe it's the humor that makes his eyes dance, maybe it's the contagious wave of energy flowing through Rusty's, but I'm tempted to flirt back. And I would if I remembered how.

"I'll go get us some drinks," he says. "What would you like?"

"A beer would be great."

I watch him stride to the bar, situated just inside the tin-roofed portion of the shanty. The bar takes up nearly three quarters of the tiny, covered space, leaving room for a handful of tables under cover.

I'm glad to be outside. The night is warm for February. And since Rusty's is on the west side of A1A, we're in a prime spot to watch the sunset.

I turn my face into the cooling breeze, breathe in the river scent and watch the amber rays of the setting sun dance over the water like nymph fingers strumming a harp.

While he waits his turn at the bar, a big-haired blonde flirts with him. I mean, of course she would. He's a good-looking guy. From this distance he appears polite, even charming, but not too…over the top.

On the makeshift dance floor—which is really just the center of the deck—sunburned men and sun-kissed women dance to the Buffett tunes. Some sway, others shuffle and stomp, moving around each other. It looks like a primal mating ritual.

Isn't that what it all boils down to?

The joining of man and woman.

Sex.

Silky longing blossoms inside me at the thought.

It's been so long.

I close my eyes against the foreign sensation. It's been a long time since I've thought of sex—sex for pleasure rather than tainted sex. Betrayal.

I open my eyes against the demons of Chet and Kally. They will not spoil my night. They will not be the invisible interlopers, haunting me, sitting at this table, making it impossible to enjoy this evening.

Across the room, Max snares my gaze as he walks toward me with six beer bottles on ice in an aluminum bucket. He smiles and that sexy feeling in the pit of my stomach unfurls again.

My hand slides down to cover my belly.

He's tall, broad-shouldered, dark and devilishly handsome. What more could a girl ask for in a man? Superficially, that is. Because I'm certainly not looking for anything deeper right now.

Persephone prods me. *Who needs more? Just follow your instincts.*

He deposits the bucket in the center of the table, then sits across from me, arranging his long-boned body in the chair. He pulls an icy bottle from the bunch, pops the cap and hands it to me. Then he helps himself and holds the bottle up to mine.

"Cheers."

As the singer transitions into "Volcano," we clink bottles and take long, slow draws of the beer.

"I like a woman who's not too dainty to drink her beer straight up like this."

I set down my bottle, feeling anything but dainty.

"I like a guy who isn't afraid to take a woman to a divey beach bar on a first date."

He smiles that smile that feels like it's made just for me. "Ah, a match made in heaven."

Then the waitress appears, breaking the spell as she shoves paper menus at us.

"I see y'all got your drinks. How 'bout some food?" She tells us her name is Stacy, rattles off the specials and says she'll be right back to take our order.

We both decide on the snow crab, one of the few catches not indigenous to the area, but too good to resist.

Max scores more points for ordering it because I can't even begin to tell you how many people—men and women alike—miss out on this sensual treat because they think it's too messy or too much work or a number of other excuses, which, in my book, do not apply.

After we place our order, the singer moves into a rowdy set of country tunes. The volume seems to increase more than a few decibels. We try to talk over it, but finally give up on conversation and people-watch, communicating without words, through glances and sexy smiles.

I like that he doesn't feel the need to talk all the time. That we can just…be.

Again, that rogue feeling creeps up on me like a creature coming up from underwater. It spirals through the pit of my stomach reminding me no matter what's happened, I'm alive.

If I was nervous or hesitant about this date before Max picked me up, I'm fine now. Relaxed, even enjoying myself— wrapped up in the music, the vibration of people stomping and dancing on the wooden deck, the exhilarating smell of the sea breeze and the magic of the setting sun bathing the river in lush pinks, cool blues and blazing oranges.

It's as if the sun is setting on a long, lonely chapter of my life and readying the stage for a new beginning.

Even if I face that new beginning alone.

Especially if I face it alone.

BY THE TIME WE FINISH our dinner, I'm light-headed from the beer and sticky from the succulent crab and drawn butter. But this doesn't stop Max from pulling me to my feet.

"Dance with me."

I shake my head. "I'm a mess. I need to wash my hands—"

"So do I. I'm a mess. You're a mess. Let's be messy together." He smiles that smile. "Besides, I like this song."

The singer's back to Buffett: "Changes in Latitude, Changes in Attitude." Since it's the theme of the night, how can I resist?

Max slides his arm around my waist and leads me to the periphery of the dance floor. Then he spins me around and the music catches me in its groove, pulls me into that sway-move people do to a tune that's neither fast nor slow, but still danceable.

We both sing that line in the song that says, *if we couldn't laugh we'd go insane*, and we laugh.

But it's the line that talks about *being able to adjust to the fall after life as you know it suddenly ends* that resonates with me.

I dance sure and light, moving farther and farther away from the problems—at least for tonight....

He takes my hand and gives me a little twirl.

When I face him again, my head is spinning and that big,

white full moon that rose so gracefully over the river suddenly has a twin. I blink several times and the two moons finally drift back together and merge into one.

I don't know if it's because of the beer or the dancing or the loud music, but I like the rush. I haven't felt the likes of this since…well, in far too long.

I'm free.

Unencumbered by past grief and the uncertainty of the future. Tonight I'm liberated and free—free to enjoy this exceptionally sexy, broad-shouldered man, no strings attached.

"I'm going to slow things down a bit." The singer strums the first strains of "Come Monday." "Grab your sweetheart on this fine Valentine's Night. It's time to get close."

Max pulls me against him.

The song is intimate—heartbreaking.

I bury my face in his shoulder and he rests his cheek on the top of my head. We sway together, barely moving.

I'm lost in the music; intoxicated by him, by the feel of his hands on me, by the smell of him, by the words of the wicked song.

I want to stay like this forever, frozen in this moment when everything is safe and fresh and new—

I love the way his hands feel as they caress my back, and I decide right then and there that I want his hands all over me.

As the song ends he puts his hand on my chin and tilts

my face up so that he's gazing right in my eyes. I let myself look at him. At the smooth, tanned line of throat visible at the open collar of his blue shirt. At the dark hair that has just the right amount of curl to it, at the way he's gazing down at me with an intensity that sends desire shimmering through me.

And I know what's going to happen before he lowers his lips to mine.

In those seconds before we kiss, in the anticipation of what comes next, I know he's not making that long drive back to Kissimmee tonight—at least not until I'm done with him.

I lean in and whisper, "Let's go."

His gaze turns razor-sharp, but he doesn't say a word, only nods.

I go to the lady's room as he pays the tab. I open my purse and take out a small blue condom packet and put it in the front pocket of my jeans. I won't allow myself to think too hard about what we're about to do. I simply wash my hands, put a few peppermint drops on my tongue and meet him on the dock that leads to the parking lot. He takes my hand and leads me toward the truck.

My heart is pounding. I know if I wait until we get back to my place, I'll find my senses right where I lost them— somewhere along that twenty-mile stretch between my front door and Rusty's.

"Let's take a walk on the beach," I say. My knees feel a

bit wobbly, but holding his hand, I manage to cross the empty road.

The moon is full and the waves crash in the distance. When we get behind the dunes, I put my arms around him. He ravishes my mouth and I tug him down onto the soft sand, letting him do as he pleases with those glorious hands.

I love the feel of his rough fingers on my smooth skin and arch under him, demanding more.

He pulls back a little. "Are you sure about this?"

I answer him by reaching for his belt buckle.

He tugs my blouse over my head, then pulls my bra down so that my breasts are naked in the moonlight. When he takes my nipple in his mouth, need courses through me, hot and ready.

As my fingers work his zipper, he pulls back again.

"Wait a minute." He's breathless. "I didn't bring anything with me."

I press my mouth to his, gently biting his lower lip.

"Ah, but I did."

He moans his appreciation.

"I love a woman who comes prepared."

"Yeah? Prove it to me."

CHAPTER 18

I wasn't purposely trying to recreate the beach scene in *From Here to Eternity*. It just sort of worked out that way.

If you've never had sex on the beach, you really must put it on your list of things to do before you die. There's something very earthy about the feel of the coarse sand and the taste of the briny air.

And yes, I'm handling it fine. Well, now that I've had a chance to digest what I did. Don't get me wrong, the sex was great—mind-blowing, in fact. But after we came down from that carnal high, things were a little awkward.

When we got back to my place, I didn't want him to come in. It seemed too personal. I needed to be alone.

Since the first thing I did when I got inside was cry and throw my purse against the wall—the leftover condoms flew out like huge squares of confetti—I'm sure it was the right call.

I don't know how long he would've stayed. And if he wanted to play the gentleman and stay the night, it would've been even more awkward asking him to leave than not inviting him in. I mean, what if someone I knew was driving by in the wee hours of the morning and spied his car in my driveway at four o'clock in the morning?

It could happen. I wouldn't put it past the Sago Beach "Dawn Patrol" to make early-morning rounds to see what they could see.

It's all about appearances.

I guess you can't escape it no matter where you are. In L.A. the appearance was physical; in Sago Beach the appearance is in how you conduct yourself.

Funny, though, the common denominator is that beneath the surface, it's all ugly.

Anyway, I digress. After I got a hold of my emotion, I made up my mind I wasn't going to feel bad about what I did. I'm a grown woman free to have sex for pleasure; we'd used condoms like two mature, responsible consenting adults.

He kissed me at the door, and said he'd call me later.

I'm not holding my breath. It was first-date sex, after all, and the original plan was to do it to get rid of him.

I finally fell asleep in the midst of giving myself props for how modern I was for having the guts to do it like a man would—no expectations, no emotions, simply taking it for what it was: A good time with a man who was great in bed.

Now it's midafternoon and I'm sitting on the couch showered and fresh in my flannel pajamas, with a book, a cup of comforting herbal tea and Miss Thang at my feet.

A humiliating chorus of the old Buffett favorite "Why Don't We Get Drunk and Screw" is playing in my head.

But I wasn't drunk. Not really. Tipsy, maybe, but not so drunk I didn't know what I was doing.

I feel like a sentinel on the watchtower, guarding my feelings, trying to keep myself from falling headfirst over the curtain wall into the sea of regret.

"So I had sex with a guy who wasn't you, Chet," I say in the direction of the guest room, because I can't bring myself to get up and say it directly to the box of his ashes.

"And yes, I'm perfectly resigned to never seeing him again. Yes. I really am. It's my choice."

Miss Thang cocks her head to one side as if she's trying to comprehend what I'm saying.

"Men have one-night stands all the time. Don't they, Chet? I have no reason to feel bad or dirty or…otherwise wrong. At least I didn't sleep with your best friend."

I take in a deep, indignant breath. Why is it that I can still smell Max—despite how I scrubbed myself—and taste him through the toothpaste and tea?

It dawns on me that the worst part of this is that I have no one to talk to about it. I don't dare tell Lonnie Sue unless I want everyone within a five-county radius to know the intimate details.

I can hear her now…. *Oh, Avril's perfectly over Chet. She's already had sex with someone else….*

And Dani has enough to figure out, taking Tommy back.

And Gilda—Oooh…I might as well tell my mother.

A knock on the door yanks me out of my mental grousing and propels Thang, barking and scrambling, to her feet. As I walk to the door, I see Kally through the glass side panels.

My heart sinks when she waves at me. I can't even pretend to not be home. I'd forgotten how people in these parts don't always call before they drop by. I make a mental note to buy curtains for the door windows.

Holding Miss Thang by the collar so she doesn't jump all over Kally, I open the door.

"Hey." She looks pale and even thinner, if that's possible. "Oh, my gosh, Avril, are you okay?"

Glancing down at my flannel PJs, I think, *Oh, you don't even know the half of it.*

I run my free hand through my mussed hair, which I didn't even bother to comb after my shower. It's dried to that semifrizz that happens when it's left to its own devices.

"I'm just…ummm…taking it easy today."

I see the two little hands wrapped around her right leg seconds before Sam peeks out from behind his mother. The likeness of Chet kicks me hard in the gut, making me inhale sudden and sharp.

Miss Thang whines and strains at my hold so that she's nearly prancing on her back legs wanting to greet the boy.

"I hope you don't mind us dropping by, but Sam and I

were in the neighborhood and he really wanted to meet—
Does the dog have a name yet?"

Subtext: *If I would've called, you would've said you were
busy. I brought the boy with me so you'll look like an ogre if you
turn us away.*

"Uh, yeah, her name is Miss Thang."

Subtext: *You're darn right I would've been busy—*

"Can I pat your doggie?" His voice is raspy and he looks
up at me with those eyes that are the same deep blue as his
father's and it takes a second for a single word to work its
way around the lump in my throat.

But somehow I manage to croak, "Sure."

Still holding Thang by her pink collar so she won't
knock the boy down in her enthusiasm, I step back and
let them in.

It only takes the dog a moment to settle down. I let go
of her and she gently licks him. His laugh is pure delight.
When Thang rolls over so he can scratch her belly, he drops
down on his knees and does a thorough job.

"Can she fetch?" he asks.

"I don't know," I say. "We haven't tried that game yet."

Sam reaches into his pocket and pulls out a twig.

"I brought her a stick." He holds it up to show me.

"I'll bet she can do it 'cause she looks real smart. Let me
show you. Here, doggie."

He tosses the stick, and it slides under the couch.

"Whoa! Whoa-whoa, bud!" Kally catches Sam by the arm as the dog barks and launches after the errant stick, pawing at the floor when she can't retrieve it from under the furniture.

"Not inside, Sam. You could break something. Now go get it and put it back in your pocket."

He looks crestfallen.

"Well, can I go outside and play with her? Please?"

Kally looks at me.

"It's fine with me. The backyard's fenced in."

Sam looks up at his mom with pleading eyes. "Pleeeease?"

Kally bends down on one knee. "Now, listen, do not go out of the backyard. Do you understand?"

He nods, excited. Then runs over to the couch to get the stick.

"No running in the house, Sam!" Kally looks exasperated. "Have you forgotten your manners?"

He stops and turns toward his mother, his head bowed. "No, ma'am. Sorry."

As he drops down on his belly to forage under the couch, Kally tells him, "Say thank you to Miss Avril for letting you play with her dog."

He scoots to his knees, shoves the stick in his pocket and examines something else he's found under the sofa. Then crumples it up in his hand.

"Thank you, Miss Avril. I really, really like your dog. I

want a doggy so bad, but Mommy says she's too sick to take care of all three of us."

Oh, my gosh. Before I can stop myself, my hand flies to my mouth.

"Sam!" The words rush out of Kally's mouth on an embarrassed gasp.

All I can do is stand there stupidly, my heart nearly breaking over a little four-year-old carrying around the burden of knowing that his mother is so sick.

"Well, that's what you said, Mommy."

"I know, sweetie. It's okay. Just go outside," Kally says, looking sheepish. "I'll come out to check on you in a few minutes."

As I walk to the back door to let Sam and the dog out, he walks up to his mother and thrusts something at her.

"Can I have this candy?" he asks.

Kally's jaw drops. She looks at me and back to what Sam gave her. "No, you don't need any candy. Go outside and play."

I hold the door open for him and as he brushes by, he looks up at me with that Chet-smile and those Chet-eyes. "Thank you, Miss Avril."

I watch him throw the stick and run out into the middle of the backyard. The dog runs, too, fetches and returns to the boy's side.

I'm frozen by a multitude of emotions revolving around the heartbreaking grief that this boy has no one else but his mother.

When I turn back to Kally, she has a funny smile on her face. "So, Avril, enjoying a little candy?"

She holds out a small blue square—I nearly die when I realize it's a wrapped condom.

"Oh, my God." I grab it from her, certain that my face is fifteen shades of purple, and crumple it in the palm of my hand as if that will make it disappear.

I must have missed it when I was picking up the things that spilled out of my purse when I threw it.

She laughs. "So who's your candy man, Av?"

I stare at her, but I don't answer. I don't know what to say. Instead, I turn around and go into the kitchen to regain my composure and stash the evidence.

I return, with two cups of tea.

"Aren't you going to tell me?" Kally asks.

"No."

She frowns. "Okay, well then, I'll change the subject. Have you given any more thought to adopting Sam when the time comes?"

I flinch at her matter-of-fact tone, as if she's asking me if I've decided what color I want to paint the living room walls. Suddenly, I wonder if this visit was even more staged than I realized. She'll bring the boy over, tell him to tell me he can't have a doggy.

Well, it's the truth, snips Persephone. *Maybe that's what she needed to do to get through to you?*

"Are you just giving up, Kally? Have you already made up your mind that you're going to die?"

That was mean. Uncalled for.

I know it, but I don't care.

Yes, you do, says Persephone.

And a little door opens and sickening emotions spill forth, proving my conscience right.

But I *don't* want to care.

"Avril, you know I have no control over that. If it were as easy as making up my mind that I wasn't going to die, then…"

"Then what? You wouldn't be here now?"

"Avril, please." She sets down her teacup and presses a shaky hand to her temple. "You know, I had this crazy thought, that you might think of me as your surrogate," Kally says.

This jolts me. Nearly blows me away and for a minute I wonder if someone told her I can't have children.

"That's an interesting way to put it."

"What do you mean?" she asks.

"I can't have kids. Did you know that?"

She shakes her head. "I knew you were trying."

"Yep. Chet and I tried for years—went through all kinds of fertility treatments and then finally the doctor pronounced us a hopeless case. So you see why it was a double insult when you and Chet only had sex once and you got pregnant."

She looks stricken, stares at her hands. "Avril, I'm sorry.

You don't know how much I wish things would've turned out differently."

"Yeah, well, they didn't so I guess there's no use beating yourself up over it."

She looks up as if I've given her hope. As if I'm letting her off the hook.

Am I?

I don't even know what I'm doing anymore.

It's just a screwed-up, unfortunate situation. Losing my husband, my marriage and my best friend—okay, former best friend—all in one leveling blow.

A part deep inside of me mourns, it cries and keens, in spite of how I stand here dry-eyed and stoic. The pain's not for Chet, but for this woman who once meant so much to me. And even though I don't want to feel this way, I realize in that moment if I could change anything it would be to somehow cross this cavern and reclaim my soul-sister.

But the bridge over that canyon is still too rickety. I'm not sure if I ventured out—even though she's met me more than halfway—that the bridge wouldn't twist and dump me into the black abyss below.

Or maybe I'm afraid I'd jump.

But at least there is a bridge, says Persephone. *A week ago there wasn't one. This isn't irreparable. Just don't take too long. You may not have the luxury of time.*

"I know you loved him first," I say.

Her eyes soften. "But he chose you, so it was no contest."

Something passes between us—an understanding? I don't know.

I motion to the couch. "Sit down. Let Sam play with the dog for a while. Let's drink our tea."

Kally smiles. "So, who's the candy man, Av? Come on, dish."

There's utter glee in her eyes and for a moment, I glimpse the old Kally.

"Do you have a boyfriend?" she asks, her eyes dancing.

"No!"

"Then what? Are condoms the hairdressers' new latex gloves?"

"Oh, my God." Unable to suppress a smile, I bury my face in my hands.

She laughs. "Tell me."

"Oh, my God, Kally, I can't believe I slept with him."

"Was it good?"

I nod.

She squeals.

Given the situation, you'd think it would be weird telling her this. But it's liberating.

"Who is he? Where did you meet him? Tell me everything!"

And I do.

For a few wonderful moments, it's just like old times. It's almost as if the cold, bitter, jaded me has stepped outside of my body and is observing the situation from a third-party perspective.

And what that cold, bitter me sees is like an old home movie of the past, of two women talking like the lifelong friends they used to be, momentarily forgetting the big pink elephant we've been dancing around since I returned.

So even if I never hear from Max again, I'd owe him a debt of appreciation for opening the door to reconciliation with Kally.

Of course, relations are far from healed, but this is a start. It's that first foot on the rickety bridge over that canyon.

"Oh, how I've missed this," Kally says, when I finally take a breath. "I've always lived vicariously through you."

"Come on. Give yourself some credit. You've done a lot better than I have. You have a business, a son…"

The old, bitter, jaded me starts to swim back into my soul, but I manage to hold her off.

"But you had Hollywood. You moved away from this place and really lived, Av. The coffee shop lets me make ends meet, but it's no gold mine, certainly not as exciting as working in the movies."

Oh, the thoughts that race through my head, round and round, trying to escape. Protests. The words: *mirage, illusion, chimera, fraud.*

"You know, Kally, all that glitters isn't necessarily gold."

She looks at me. Really looks at me.

"All my life I've felt one step out of sync. Even my name was a little off—Kally. Do you know how often in my life I've been called Kelly?" She gestures to herself. "I mean look at me. I'm a mess. I've always been a mess. You, on the other hand, have always held it together. Effortlessly. It just came naturally."

She laughs, but it's a dry, humorless sound.

I start to protest, but she silences me with a hand.

"Avril, even when things don't work out for you, they work out. Somehow, you always manage to be okay, to come out on top. I'm *not* feeling sorry for myself and I don't want your pity—I don't want *anyone's* pity. But I know in my bones, in my heart, what's going to happen in a very short while."

She chokes and covers her mouth with her hand. Tears cloud her eyes, and her arm slides down into her lap as if she doesn't have the strength to hold it up.

"It stinks. It really stinks because I can't do a damn thing to change it. And Sam's the one who'll be left to go on. He's just a little boy. If he goes into foster care, he'll have no chance in this world."

My eyes tear, too, and I blink to stave off the flood.

"What I'm asking…and after what's happened, I know I have no right to ask anything of you…but please consider giving Sam a home. Teach him how to be strong and survive. Because you're a survivor, Avril. Will you do that for him?"

I'M SITTING AT MY COMPUTER researching leukemia feeling more confused than enlightened by what I've found. There's so many different kinds of leukemia—acute vs. chronic; lymphoid vs. myeloid; lymphocytic vs. myelogenous. I have no idea what it all means or which variety Kally has. She told me, but it's all so technical, I can't remember.

It's a welcome break when the phone rings. I expect it to be my mother and I really want to talk to her about Kally and Sam and this heinous disease that's taking over Kally's body.

But it's not Mama.

"I wanted to send you roses," says Max. "But I decided that would be too cliché."

I hate myself for the way my body reacts to his voice: a mixture of awareness and heat in vulnerable places and a sense of relief that I had no idea I'd feel hearing him on the line.

"Hi, Max."

I don't want to be relieved. I want to be smug and cynical, telling myself all men are alike.

And who knows, maybe he is like all the others. It's still early in the game.

"Since I didn't send flowers, I thought I'd do the old-fashioned thing and call you and say I had a great time last night. When can I see you again?"

I minimize the computer screen and lean back in my chair, stretching my legs out in front of me.

"I thought guys ran fast when a woman gave it up on the first date? You know, the challenge is over."

He chuckles low and sexy, and I shudder remembering the heat of his breath on my neck and the weight of his body on mine.

"I have no idea what you're talking about. Last night *was* our third date. If you count the flight from L.A. it was our fourth."

I love the sound of his voice, deep, rich and earthy.

"Nope. The flight from L.A. definitely doesn't count. And even if it did, how do you arrive at Rusty's being our third date?"

"Number one was coffee at the diner. Number two was when I helped you move your furniture—"

Has he been talking to Lonnie Sue?

"Whoa. Wait a minute. If you call moving furniture a date then I don't think I want to date you."

He's silent for a few beats and I wonder if he thinks I'm serious. I wonder if I'm serious. Because I've been telling myself it didn't matter if I talked to him again and here I am feeling all jittery and giddy over his call.

"Okay. Then I get a do-over for date number two."

Oh, good. I finally exhale. *He gets my humor. A good sense of humor has always been high on my sexy list.*

"A do-over, huh? What did you have in mind?"

"How about if you come inland and let me show you around the grand metropolis of Kissimmee?" he says.

"Sounds tempting, but there's one problem."

"What's that?"

"I don't have a car. I sold it before I left L.A."

"I could pick you up and bring you back."

That would get old really fast—an hour each direction would add up to four hours of commute time if he picked me up, drove me back, brought me home and went home. "No. I can't in good conscience let you drive all that way."

"I wouldn't have offered if I minded."

"I'm getting a car soon. Like tomorrow, if I can gear myself up for it. I've been putting it off because I can't think of many things I hate worse than dickering for wheels—well, other than moving furniture on a date."

He laughs and my toes curl at the earthy sound.

"How about some help?" he offers. "It just so happens I have a talent for bringing car salesmen to their knees. It'll be our second date."

"Oookaaay, sliding down the date hierarchy from furniture-moving to car-buying. This doesn't bode well, Mr. Wright. I think I see a pattern developing here."

"God, I hope so." His voice deepens a few shades, sending a quicksilver rush coursing though my veins.

"I hope the pattern is very close to last night—especially our walk on the beach."

I actually blush. I press my free hand to my left cheek. My palm is cool against the heat of my skin. I'm way out of my league here. I want to ask him if he's a player—*Is sex all you want from me, Max?*

It dawns on me that I wouldn't mind if he said, *Yes, that's all I'm after.*

But I can't ask him that, and the good girl in me searches for a way to get on safer ground.

He must sense my hesitation because he says, "So I guess that means that after we car shop, I'll have to spring for dinner. Would that be a suitable second date?"

"That's more like it. But you know, since it's only date number two, I can't sleep with you."

"Well, in that case, let's hurry up and get this second-date business over with so we can move on to number four— because I can't get you out of my mind."

I want to ask him, *Why? What does a good looking guy like him want with a damaged woman like me?* But he doesn't know about me and all my baggage—

"I'll pick you up at five, okay?"

"Okay. Bye."

Oh, God.

After we hang up, I have to catch my breath. I'm in way, way over my head. Swimming against a rip current that's much too strong for me—I haven't dated since the seventh grade. More years than I care to count.

Swim parallel to the shore, Persephone reminds me. *You'll be fine.*

"Easy for you to say."

In that instant I panic. I can't do this. Max thinks I'm someone else—a sultry, carefree, let's-have-sex-on-the-beach kind of woman, but that's not me. I can't pretend anymore.

I've played the good girl for so many years, it's pretty much the only role I know how to play.

The only role I've ever been offered.

Except for now, quips Persephone. *It's easier to blame others for all the years that have slipped away than to take responsibility yourself, isn't it? From here on out you've got no one else but yourself to blame.*

Resentment, hot and sour, burns the back of my throat, a bitter note for always playing it safe. For never breaking out of the part and taking chances.

My gaze lights on the closet where I stashed the box of Chet's ashes. I jerk open the louvered door and take out the box.

"I'm too young to be your grieving widow, Chet. I'm too young to shut myself away. And frankly, you don't deserve that from me after what you did."

I choke on the last words, and that's when the tears come. Like a flash flood, all the grief and guilt and longing and confusion I've harbored since he died pour out.

"How could you do this to me? To us? To Kally...and Sam?"

I actually pull my arm back, ready to slam the box on the floor, not caring if he goes up in a big cloud of dust.

But something stops me. I fall to my knees, hugging my husband's remains to my chest.

"How could you make such a mess out of things and just leave? We had unfinished business, Chet. We had issues that we'll never solve, and you have a son who's about to lose everything. He's just a little boy, Chet. He didn't do anything to deserve this. But you—you're just gone. Gone like you always were. Leaving everyone else behind."

As I cry, my thoughts race from how my life was impacted by growing up without a father, to how grateful I am to have my mother, to wondering if the distance between Chet and me would've ended in divorce, to imagining Kally and Chet together.

I think that if I just force myself to visualize his night with Kally—every detail, with cinemalike clarity—the sadness will fade like a movie gives way to the closing credits.

I know it sounds a little sick, wanting to picture your husband making love to another woman. But I need to put this to rest. I suppose a part of me hopes that after I shine a bright, hard light on it, it'll be easier to understand.

Just like when Chet's producer told me about the accident. Told me Chet died on impact. That, yes, he probably had a few frightening moments when he realized his parachute wasn't opening, but it was all over within seconds.

Knowing the truth made it a easier to digest and in some ways it prepared me for the very public aftermath.

Since he was a minor celebrity in L.A., a reporter did a story on why people are drawn to extreme sports, saying thrill junkies were basically rebelling against the rules.

Is that what happened that night he made love to Kally? Was he simply breaking the rules? Did the danger-zone adrenaline kick in? Or after her mother's funeral did he simply feel his own mortality?

I'll never know. Just like I'll never know whether he thought about me when he fell into her arms? Whether either of them hesitated and considered even for one split second the potential impact this would have on everyone involved?

Especially the little boy that will be left behind.

The credits are rolling in this movie in my mind, but I can't picture him with her. Instead something else is illuminated: Kally didn't cause the demise of my marriage. Chet and I were in trouble long before his night with her. We'd grown up and apart. Even though I loved him, I have to admit, I didn't like the man he'd become—Mr. Hollywood, all glitz and glamour, shiny slick and lacking in substance. It wasn't my dream we went to pursue, it was his. But maybe I shouldn't blame him for having a dream of his own. After all, Hollywood life is a classic example of survival of the fittest.

Knowing what you know now, says Persephone, *if you had the chance to do everything over, would you marry him again?*

Would you so willingly let him drag you away from paradise and into the bowels of hell?

"Hollywood was definitely hell, but I don't know if you'd call Sago Beach paradise—"

Don't change the subject.

"No, I wouldn't marry him. Not if things turned out this way."

It's so strange. I'm not devastated by this revelation. It's as if someone opened the cage door and a captive bird flew free.

That captive bird is my heart.

I glance down at the box of his ashes and I know I must put Chet to rest. Only then will I be able to make my peace with Kally and set the whole ugly situation right in my heart. Only then will I be able to move on.

CHAPTER 19

I always wanted an Infiniti G35 coupe—a red one—and since I have the money to buy it, I decided why not.

For the first time in my life I was going to get exactly what I wanted without second-guessing myself.

That's why I ended up buying the Infiniti FX35 SUV in sapphire. When I was shopping, I realized that a coupe wasn't practical. I have a dog. I'm single and I may need to haul things—don't ask me what, but this way I won't have to impose on anyone.

Since I paid cash—and, yes, it was surreal to walk into a dealership and write a check for five figures—I had an easy time negotiating a good deal.

Yes, you heard me right, I negotiated the deal. Max was there for support, but I decided before he picked me up that this was my baby. Chet had always been the one to buy the cars we drove and they were always what he wanted.

This one is totally mine.

And it feels wonderful.

After the deal is sealed, we swing back by my place to

drop off his truck and go celebrate at the Mango Tree, over in Cocoa Beach.

The restaurant has always reminded me of a plantation home in the South Pacific—or at least what I imagine one to be. It's a feast for the senses even before we set foot in the building. We walk through lavish gardens of colorful flowers, foliage and whimsical topiaries. In the middle of everything, a beautiful waterfall splashes into a Japanese koi pond. It's like an enchanted wonderland and it sets a good tone for the night.

Max takes my hand and leads me inside. We're greeted by the silky sound of piano music. The décor is eclectic with Persian rugs and large cushioned wicker chairs. On the far wall is an iridescent butterfly collection hung above a spectacular saltwater aquarium.

Everywhere I look I see original works of art, stained-glass accents and treasures that reveal themselves as I glance around.

The good thing about a beach town is anything dressier than bathing suits and shorts is appropriate for a "fancy" restaurant. So my slacks and twin sweater set blend in fine.

The maître d' seats us at a cozy window table, and as Max orders a bottle of wine, I listen to the pianist switch from "Some Enchanted Evening" to a classical piece I don't recognize. Honestly, after the casual air of Rusty's on Valentine's Day, I wasn't expecting something this fancy tonight. This guy is full of surprises.

Maybe it's the cynical pessimist in me that's surfaced with all that's happened over the past year, but the thought *too good to be true* springs to mind. I push it away, refusing to put the cart before the horse.

This is just a date.

Only the *second date* according to Max.

But still it feels like much more and that makes me feel a little vulnerable. I have to admit, I like Max's gentle persistence. I like his sense of humor and the way he makes me smile. He's forward, but not pushy, and I think if I told him to stop, that he was moving too fast, he would back off.

In fact, he hasn't done or said anything that I haven't encouraged—and, I must confess, I've liked it.

So maybe what I like the most about him is this different side of me that he brings out.

"So, Max," I say after the server has poured the wine and left us to look over the menus. "Isn't this driving back and forth all that way getting a little old?"

He quirks a mischievous brow. "Are you asking me to move in with you?"

"No!" I swat his arm. "Are you ever serious?"

His eyes darken to an intensity that makes the brown appear almost black in the candlelight.

"I can be serious when the situation gets… serious. I've never had a problem with that. When it was…right."

The innuendo steals my words, and I feel flustered and

anxious. I'm not sure what he's getting at. If he's even getting at *anything*.

In turn, my wondering if he's thinking serious in relationship terms makes me feel stupid, an amateur in a game she has no business playing right now.

Still, even against my better judgment, I have to ask, "Max, why me? Why do you keep traveling all this way to see me…?"

For a moment, his brow knits in confusion. Then he shrugs and raises his glass to me.

"Why not you, Avril? Do you want me to stop?"

No.

The answer floods through me so fast it's jarring. I don't even have to think about it. When I think too much things get complicated—with the *what-ifs* and *what-abouts* and all the unknowns that could sideline me if I let them.

I shake my head, unable to speak, and a sexy smile barely turns up the corners of his lips before he leans in and kisses me.

"Why you?" he says. "Because I like how you're strong and vulnerable all at the same time. Because you strike me as someone who is made of small-town-substance, rather than big-city-flash. Because judging from the greeting at the airport and the way your friends gathered around you when we moved you into your house, your relationship with your family is obviously important to you. And besides, I told you I was damn curious to find out exactly how a *Beauty Operator to the Stars* was going to function in a place like Sago Beach."

I'm stunned. Speechless. All warm inside because a man like Max would find value in such small, seemingly insignificant things.

The very insignificant things that were missing from my life in California.

I have no idea what this means or where Max and I are going. The only thing I know is that I don't want to think about it too hard tonight. I want to sit back and live in the moment—because all too soon, I'll be back in the place where I have to think about what comes next.

We place our orders—sea bass for me, the fillet cooked rare for Max. He insists I try a glass of the sauvignon blanc since the bottle of red will overpower the delicate fish.

It feels good to be fussed over. But though it's nice, I'm not completely at ease being the full-time taker. I turn the focus on him.

"So tell me about you."

He toys with his wineglass.

"What do you want to know?"

"Have you ever been married?"

He nods. "Once. How did you put it—that was another life?"

"Touché."

We're silent for a minute and I realize he's not so comfortable having others ask the questions.

"If you tell me about yours, I'll tell you about mine," I offer. "Deal?"

He looks at me in a way that makes me wonder if he's assessing the possible fallout of telling too much. At this point in the relationship the other person can be anything we want them to be in our minds. But if this is going to be… more—and by calling, he indicated he wanted more, on some level—we're going to have to open up and share more of ourselves.

"Deal," he says.

"Okay, you go first."

He looks as if he might protest, then smiles at me like I've beat him at his own game.

"Fair enough," he says. "Married for five years. We met in college. She married me for all the wrong reasons and cheated on me. Divorced for three years. Who was this other Mr. Right that Tanya was talking about at the diner the other day?"

"Not so fast," I say. "Tell me about L.A."

He refills our glasses. "After the divorce I needed to get away from all the gossip and speculation and moved to California to manage the west-coast division of the company I work for."

"What kind of business is it?"

"Nope. I've answered two questions." He grins. "It's your turn."

"Fair enough."

"So who's the other Mr. Right in your life?"

I take a deep breath and leap off the high dive. I tell him about Chet.

"I'm pretty screwed up and damaged, Max. I have an irrational fear of flying—as you saw that day on the plane—and I'm not nearly as adventurous as I thought I was. So I'm giving you your out right now if you want."

He shakes his head. "Why did you leave California?"

"You first. Why did you leave? Actually, *have* you left or are you going back?"

"I came back to Florida because I was finally ready. My ex has moved on. She's remarried and…well, Florida is home. I missed it. L.A. made me feel kind of empty. So, there were some business issues I needed to deal with in Kissimmee and here I am. As for going back to L.A., that remains to be seen, but probably not. At least not permanently."

I raise my brows at him.

"Let's just say, my company allows me a lot of flexibility. Now you, why did you leave?"

I think about this for a minute. There's not an easy answer to the question. It goes deeper than losing Chet and coming home to Mama.

"Because for me, it was a land where dreams were only facades. Because I know Sago Beach's rhythms, which doesn't mean I only like what's predictable. No, it's more that I like what's *real*."

"You asked me *why you*? That's why, Avril."

A gentle thrill rushes through me like a whisper, and I realize I could get used to this feeling. That scares me.

It crosses my mind that if the pre-third-date sex didn't scare him off, maybe my spilling the rest of the ugly story would. If he's considering getting involved with me, isn't it only fair to tell him what he's bargaining for?

"Although, since I've been home," I say, "nearly everything I thought was real has proved to be a sham."

"What do you mean?"

I run my finger around the rim of my wineglass, trying to compose my words.

"About four days after I got back I found out that my husband had an affair with my best friend before he died—well, I don't know if you'd call one night of sex an affair. Actually, I don't even know if you'd call what they shared *sex*. As much as I hate to admit it, they made love. He had feelings for her even if he wasn't madly in love with her. But I suppose since it happened, he wasn't madly in love with me anymore, either. Anyway, their one night together produced a child. I've met the boy and Kally, my friend, wants me to adopt him because she has leukemia—"

I realize I'm rambling. "Uggh—sorry, probably more than you wanted to know. Remember, you can bow out now if you want."

His face softens.

"Thanks for the out, but I think I'll stick around and take my chances."

Oh.

My stomach flips. Much to my dismay it actually does a giddy, girly three-sixty.

I press my hand to my belly to stop the sensation. And as I do, all I can think of is, *Oh, my God, I'm such a slut. I'm going to sleep with him on the second date.*

THE NEXT MORNING, I arrive at work an hour before we're supposed to open so I can show off my new wheels. Mama's the only one there and I'm glad we have this time alone.

I take her for a ride around the block and after we've sufficiently *oohed* and *aahed* over the car, she tells me to park in the empty spot under the carport, next to the T-Bird.

She's just about to get out of the car when I say, "Mama, I think it's time to scatter Chet's ashes."

She shuts the door again. "I think that's a good idea. Did you have a date in mind?"

"I was thinking maybe next week. Let's look at the appointment schedule and see when looks good."

"You just pick a date, honey, and we'll make it work." She

reaches out and takes my hand and we sit in the quiet of the car for a few minutes.

"I was thinking I'd invite Kally and Sam to join us."

Her voice and expression are neutral. "Is that what you want?"

I nod. "Yes, I think so. I think that's what I need to do get some closure out of this...."

This what? This mess? This ordeal? I don't know that there's even an adequate word for *this*.

But maybe that's for the best.

Words are labels.

And labels make things a little too permanent. I want *this* to run its course and go away. Realistically, maybe it can never completely go away, but I want to make my peace with Kally and Sam—especially Sam.

"I've been thinking about Sam a lot lately, and I decided I want to continue the child support payments that Chet was making."

Mama's lips tighten into a thin line.

"Did she ask you for money?"

"No, she didn't. She said she was barely making ends meet at Lady Marmalade's, but that was in the course of conversation. It wasn't a hint for money. Mama, she's too proud to ask anyone for help. With the insurance money I received after Chet died, I have more than enough to be comfortable. Maybe if I help Kally along now, she'll be more comfortable finding another guardian for Sam."

Don't ask me why I think this is logical—maybe it's because it makes me feel as if I'm doing something to help the boy since I can't give him a home.

"Are you sure that's what you want her to do? I was thinking maybe Sam was the reason you decided on the SUV over the sports car? That maybe you were thinking of adopting the boy?"

"No! I mean, I don't know." I cross my arms over the front of me and hit my elbow on the steering wheel. "I got the SUV because I liked it. Because of the dog."

Mama doesn't look convinced, but she finally says, "Okay, well, helping Kally out with child support is a noble thing to do, Avril. I think it's very generous."

I draw in a deep breath.

"I'm not trying to be noble. I'm trying to do what's right. When I go out and buy a new car with money from Sam's father's life insurance policy, I think it's only right that I do something for the boy."

When we go back inside, Gilda, Lonnie Sue and Dani are there.

We look at the car and we're back inside for less than a minute when I sense something's up with Lonnie Sue. She's acting more squirrelly than usual and has a certain air about her that makes me set down my cup of coffee, put my hands on my hips, and say, "What?"

She glances at Dani, who is putting on her makeup, then back at me like she wants to tell me something, but at the last second decides against it. Instead she motions to the back room, where she appears a moment later with Mama in tow.

"Gilda already knows and she's distracting Dani," she whispers. "We have to be quick."

"Why, what's going on?" Mama demands.

Lonnie Sue's face goes pale. I glance at Mama who obviously doesn't know any more than I do.

"I need your help in staging an intervention with Dani. We have got to get her away from that dirtbag of a man she calls a husband. I can't believe she's taking him back. I had Sid investigate Tommy and he's still screwing around with that bimbo she caught him with." The words spill out in a breathless stream. "She's a stripper at an all-nude club over in Cocoa Beach. Can you believe that? A stripper?" Lonnie Sue looks like she smells something foul. "Stage name's Lola LaFuenta. Real name's Junie Myers. Sid seems to think lap dances ain't the only thing she's selling, if you know what I mean. Must be giving Tommy a bulk discount. I have no hang-ups with sex and nudity, but when a stripper bitch goes messing with someone's husband—a friend's husband—I get mad."

"Oh, my Lord." Mama finally finds her voice. "Okay, how do you want to handle it?"

"Thank God she's got the last customer of the day," says Lonnie Sue. "Let's wait until after we close and then we can't let her go home."

"She can stay at my house," I offer.

Mama shakes her head. "She can stay with me up in the apartment. I'll just take her right up the stairs and tuck her into bed in Avril's room. Because that's what friends do. They take care of each other in hard times."

"What color hair dye do you need, Dani?" Gilda's voice booms. "I'll get it for you."

Gilda appears in the door and makes an almost imperceptible head motion in Dani's direction.

"All rightie, girls, we'd better get this place ready to open," Mama returns in an extra loud voice as she leaves the room.

"I know this isn't easy," I whisper to Lonnie Sue, "but after Dani sorts everything out, I know she'll appreciate it."

"I hope so." She studies me through her heavily mascaraed lashes. "So you wouldn't be mad if I had your man investigated behind your back?"

"Not if you found out something I needed to know."

A slow smile spreads over Lonnie Sue's face, and a sick feeling blooms in my belly. I cross my arms over the front of me as if they can shield me from the truth.

"What?"

Lonnie Sue looks more like herself again. So at least the news isn't bad—at least not as bad as the bomb she's going to drop on Dani.

"I guess I got a little concerned about you, too. I started thinking it through and decided after all you've been through and seeing how you've come into some money since Chet's death. Well, I just wanted to make sure he wasn't the sort to take you for a ride and break your heart—"

"I'd have to give him my heart before he could break it."

"You may not be giving him your heart, but you're certainly giving him something else."

She cocks a *challenge me and I'll broadcast all* brow and I want to crawl into a drawer and hide. Once we've established that, her smile returns.

"Clean record."

"That's a good start," says Gilda from the doorway where I didn't know she was listening. "What else?"

She joins us.

"Thirty-six years old. Divorced—once. Married for five years. Been apart for about three years. So he's had enough time to get past the rebound stage."

"He told me all this," I say.

"No kids, though, which is probably a good thing so's not to tie him to his ex and complicate things."

Kids.

The thought hits me square in the solar plexus. It's a pain

so sharp, it makes me draw in a quick breath. Not that it should matter, but he's still young enough to have kids if he wants them.

Despite all the other personal information I spilled last night, I didn't tell him that I can't have kids.

The slow-burning realization sinks in that if I date men my age, this is an issue that will keep coming up. One more reason to not get attached, because the child issue is bound to matter in the end.

"Here's the best part." Lonnie Sue reaches for me, positively ready to burst. "Are you ready for this?"

She squeezes my hands and Gilda grabs a hold of my arm as if she can hardly wait for the revelation.

"He's rich, Avril. And I don't mean just a little rich. He comes from the Wright cattle family in Kissimmee. They're like the bovine royalty of the southeast. We're talking old money that goes way back. What do y'all think of that?"

Gilda and Lonnie Sue both talk at once, all excited as if I've just won the lottery or that guy from the Publishers Clearing House Sweepstakes just walked into the room with balloons and a big check with my name on it.

It shouldn't matter if a man is rich or working class. It shouldn't matter if a woman is fertile or barren. But as I watch them talking ninety to nothing, celebrating what they see as my good fortune, it's clear that it matters, that a person's worth can increase or decrease because of things like this.

DURING ONE OF THE rare slow moments when none of us has customers and Dani is over at the diner eating her lunch and Lonnie Sue is out running an errand, Mama says, "So, this Max is a good guy?"

"What? You heard he's rich? I'm sure Lonnie Sue couldn't contain herself. I hope that in light of the bad news she has for Dani, she showed a little consideration."

"Lonnie Sue didn't tell me, smarty pants. Gilda did."

"Yeah, smarty pants." Gilda walks by and gives my shoulder a squeeze. "And it doesn't matter how much money he has, it's how he treats you."

"That's right." Mama looks pensive. "I don't want you to get hurt again, baby."

Oh, boy. I brace myself for a lecture on abstinence or at least safe sex. But all she says is, "Maybe the three of us can have dinner sometime?"

Mama smiles at me, and suddenly things feel more in focus.

"That would be nice," I say. "I'll mention it to him."

"I want to see him again, too," says Gilda before she disappears into the back room.

"In due time," I call after her, but she must not hear me because she doesn't argue.

About fifteen minutes later my cell phone rings. I glance at the number and see that it's Max.

"Hi there," I say.

"Well, hello." I can hear the smile in his voice.

"You didn't tell me you were rich," I say.

There's a pause on his end of the line. "You never asked."

"I guess I didn't."

"How'd you hear that piece of vicious gossip?"

I try to balance the small phone on my shoulder as I tear off pieces of foil in preparation for my next appointment, but end up getting a crick in my neck.

"Lonnie Sue is sleeping with the sheriff and sweet-talked him into investigating you. Just another day in Sago Beach."

"So does this change things between us? I don't know if I told you, but my ex married me for my money and was terribly disappointed. Of course, it could've had something to do with the fact that her stodgy, rich New England family thought my coming from cow money was beneath her. We learned the hard way that blue blood and cowboys just don't mix."

I'm a little taken aback by what he's told me. My heart aches for him, for the pain he must have felt realizing the person who promised to love him for better or worse wasn't the person he married.

It happened to me, too. Another common thread between us. I know how hard it must have been to get past it.

My mouth goes dry as I remember what I need to share with him. But he speaks first.

"In light of this revelation, does it mean they'll charge me more next week if I take you to that street dance they've been advertising on that big banner stretched across Main Street?"

I give up on tearing foil and sit down on the edge of my station chair. "Are you asking me to the dance?"

He laughs and the sound unleashes that old familiar serge of electricity deep in my belly. "I figured I'd better get a jump on the other hometown boys before they start filling up your dance card.

"God knows they've had that sign up there long enough. You don't already have a date, do you?"

"Sure I do, you just asked me, but I need to tell you something—"

"I know you're not going to say you can't dance. What's up?"

I swallow hard, feeling stupid telling him over the phone, but if it matters like I'm sure it will, I don't want to watch him stand up and walk away like Chet did.

"I can't have kids."

There, I said it. I hold my breath waiting for his answer. He's silent for a few beats longer than is comfortable.

I'm just about to tell him he doesn't have to comment, that I'll understand if he wants a clean break, but he says, "I guess that solves the birth control issue. So we're all set for the dance?"

I want to cry happy tears. Tears of relief that this secret that's weighted me down and damaged my life is out. I know that he might change his mind once he thinks about it. We may never take this relationship to the next level, but for now…let's just take it one day at a time.

"It's a date."

As I hang up the phone I feel giddy, light like a breath that's escaped a sigh. *He asked me to the dance*. I haven't been asked to a dance since I was in high school.

For the rest of the day, I focus on the good, pulling myself back to center when my mind wanders to unpleasant things. The only way to get through it all is to take it one step at a time.

All too soon it's time to face the "Dani Intervention."

We all hang around while she finishes her last appointment, a quick haircut. I'm surprised she doesn't question us because each of us is acting a little cagey.

After Mama turns over the Closed sign on the front door, she says, "Dani, honey, sit down, we need to talk to you."

She looks a little concerned, but obviously has no idea what's in store.

"Dani, don't be mad at me…." Lonnie Sue's voice trails off in an uncertain nervousness that I've never heard from her before. Somehow she manages to report all the things that Sid found when he investigated Tommy.

Dani stands and there's a look of death on her face I didn't know she was capable of.

"Lonnie Sue," she growls the words through gritted teeth.

"I'm only going to say this once: Stay out of my business. I don't need you checking up on my husband for me."

Mama walks over ready to play ref. Gilda and I glance at each other and I know what she's thinking—we don't need a replay of what happened last time Dani confronted Tommy's cheating. We don't need any more ugly going on in this house of beauty.

"Dani," Mama says as if she means business. "Honey, if he's having sex with a prostitute, it's not healthy for you. You could catch all kinds of nasty diseases."

Dani starts crying and bows her head, looking a little embarrassed.

"Dani," Mama continues, "I want you and Renie to stay here with me until you get things figured out. And honey, if you need some time—"

Dani straightens. "No, ma'am, I don't need anything. I'm fine." She glares at Lonnie Sue. "I just want *her* word that she's going to mind her own-damn business and not spread this all over town."

Lonnie Sue looks devastated. "Dani, on my honor, I promise you that I won't breathe a word of this. As long as you give us your word that you'll file for divorce from Tommy. Do we have a deal?"

CHAPTER 20

A week to the day later, Mama, Kally, Sam and I gather at the Sago Marina on a cool, cloudy day to board the boat I chartered to sprinkle Chet's ashes.

He always said he wanted to be cremated and have his ashes scattered in the ocean. I will honor his wishes, even though I don't understand them.

When I die, I want to be one with the earth again. Because even though the soul supposedly leaves the body when you die, I believe there's still an essence of the person that remains. Like how the wick of a candle still glows orange for a few seconds after you blow out the flame. I believe you should let the essence dissipate naturally rather than forcing it out. Chet never agreed. In fact, the thought of slowly dissipating souls used to creep him out.

"When you're dead, you're dead," he used to say. "I don't want to think about hanging around in some creepy state of limbo. Just fire me up and scatter me in the Atlantic."

Maybe more than the dissipating soul theory, I was attached to the idea of having our final resting place together. Side-by-side. Rather than becoming dust in the wind and getting scattered from here to Daytona.

How symbolic. Isn't that what happened to our relationship? Hasn't it been scattered in bits and pieces between California and Sago Beach?

Whatever. This is what he wanted.

I'll honor his wishes.

Kally looks pale and drawn and is coughing like she has bronchitis. She's strong through the ceremony, which only lasts long enough to say a few words about Chet. I considered getting a minister to come and perform an official ceremony, but Chet wasn't a religious man. It would've been pointless.

I brought a photo of him, and Kally tries to explain to Sam that this boat trip is to honor his father, but the boy is more interested in driving the boat—as a four-year-old should be. The captain graciously acommodates him while I say a few words about Chet being a driven sports reporter, a loyal companion and friend—I can't bring myself to say *husband* because of the circumstances—and I look Kally right in the eyes when I say I forgive him.

"I forgive you, too, Mama," I add.

Kally looks as if she's holding her breath and waiting. But I stand there for a moment gazing at her, recalling what this woman once meant to me.

Kally Fuller. My friend. My soul-sister.

"And I forgive you, too, Kally."

Her expression is heartbreaking. Then she closes her eyes, bows her head and weeps silently as Mama helps me sprinkle the ashes into the Atlantic Ocean. It's weird watching what remains of Chet trail through the water. As I watch the ashes catch the current and drift out to sea, a sense of relief washes over me.

I could swear I hear Persephone whisper, *You're going to be all right. It's time for me to leave, but it's time for you to get on with your life.*

WHEN WE DOCK at the marina, Kally is almost too worn out to carry herself out of the boat.

"Are you okay?" I ask her after she's finally standing on the dock.

"I'm just really tired."

"Your cough sounds worse," Mama says. "Have you seen a doctor about it?"

"I have an appointment the day after tomorrow—" The coarse, raspy cough doubles her over.

Mama pats her on the back and shoots me a what-are-we-going-to-do look as she walks Kally over to a bench about five yards away.

Sam is over at the edge of the dock. I walk over and take him by the hand. He teeters on the edge and looks up at me a little startled. I wonder how Kally will be able to look after him and take care of herself, too…when that time comes.

"Whatcha doin'?" I ask the boy.

"Feeding the fish." He pulls his hand out of mine, shoves it into his pocket and pulls out a fistfull of bread crumbs the boat captain gave him onboard when they were feeding the fish from the boat. "See that big one there? He's really hungry. Watch."

He pulls out a few crumbs, holds his fist over the water and opens it. Sure enough, the big fish beats the small ones to the punch.

Sam claps his hands in glee. "See? He's the hungriest fish in the sea."

"I think you're right. Hey, Sam, how would you like to go to the beach with me today?"

He glances back at Kally, who is now sitting on a bench leaning against Mama. "Is Mommy coming, too?"

"I think she might like some time to rest. So how about just you and me? We can get ice cream."

He sticks his hands in his pockets and shrugs, unconvinced. I drop down to one knee. "I've never been fishing off the pier before. Have you?"

He shakes his head, and his eyes brighten a little.

"I think between the two of us, you and I could figure it out together. Whaddya say? Will you take me fishing, Sam?"

Again, he glances at Kally. "I have to ask my mommy."

I stand up. "Let's go ask her together."

I offer him my hand and he takes it as we walk over to the bench.

"Hey, Mommy, Avril wants me to take her fishing. Can I? If you say yes, you can go home and sleep."

Kally lifts her head and gives me a questioning glance. "Since when do you fish?"

I shrug. "There's a first time for everything."

Kally stares at me for a long time, her eyes welling. As she reaches up and brushes away the tears, she whispers, "Thank you, my friend. Thank you."

I FOLLOW MAMA AS SHE drives Kally to her apartment over in Cocoa Beach. As we get her settled, Mama and I try to talk her into going to the emergency room, but she's adamant about waiting for her appointment.

"I get like this sometimes," she says, "then I bounce back. I'd be better off sleeping than sitting in the emergency room all night."

I feel uneasy about it, but she insists. To prove as much, she places a call to Surfer Boy—um, Zane—herself and makes arrangements for him to pick up Sam at three o'clock at my house.

"Can I see the dog?" Sam asks, jumping up and down.

So after we drop off Mama, we swing back by my house to get Miss Thang and take her with us to the pier.

"Do I get to put worms on the hook?" Sam asks, happily ensconced in his carseat in the backseat, with Thang riding shotgun next to him.

"Mmmmm," is the only answer I can give.

Worms? On hooks? Oh, that's right. He's only four years old. I can't let him bait the hook. So that means I have to— Uggggh! I'm a girly-girl. I'm into hair and makeup and pretty, girly things. So much for thinking this through. I'd seen signs on the pier advertising fishing poles for rent, but didn't think about bait. I didn't have a father to take me fishing and teach me these things—

It hits me that neither does Sam. As much as I hate to admit it, to play into Kally's negative self-talk, after seeing her so weak, he might not have a mother much longer, either. I'd never seen her so...fragile. So totally and completely whipped. Sure she'd looked frail before, all bruised skin and bones and dark circles, but she never was so out of it that she'd forgotten Sam to the point that he could've gotten hurt. He could've so easily fallen in the water this morning, and I'm sure if Kally would've realized it, she would've never forgiven herself.

I glance in the rearview mirror at the little blond boy with the big blue eyes—at the spitting image of my husband and a voice deep inside of me says, *Avril, he needs you. And maybe you need him, too.*

The voice isn't Persephone. It's my own.

But I can't quite go there...yet? Ever?

Oh, I don't know.

"Hey, Sam, I've never baited a hook before. Will you teach me?"

"I don't know how, either."

"Maybe we can learn together?"

"'Kay."

"YOU? BAITED A HOOK the other day?" Max wraps his arms around me in the middle of the makeshift dance floor at the Founder's Day dance. "With a minnow?"

The band plays a slow, sensual, heartbreaking version of Chris Isaak's "Wicked Game," and the two of us sway together.

"Yes, I most certainly did."

Main Street is strung with thousands of little white lights, transforming it into a fairyland. A warm breeze sweeps in off the ocean, and I tilt my face up to breathe in the scent of the sea mixed with the aroma of street fair food—grilled burgers, funnel cakes and beer. This devastatingly perfect night takes my breath away.

"I'll have to see that before I believe it. Can we run down to the pier for a demonstration between dances?"

"Nope. Sorry, that was a one-time performance. Plus, I got my nails done for this hot date I have tonight. I wouldn't want to ruin my manicure."

I lean back and pretend to flick his nose, but he catches my finger between his teeth and gives me a playful bite that sends white-hot currents of awareness pulsing through me.

"Hot date, huh? I like the sound of that." He pulls me close and kisses me, right there in front of the whole town, but I don't care. Let them talk. As the singer sings about *wanting to fall in love*, for the first time in my life, I want to give them something to talk about.

All I know is that I like the way he tastes and the way his arms feel around me. I melt into the warmth of him as the singer sings the part about the world being on fire and *no one can save me but you*. I want to stay like this forever.

But the music ends all too soon, giving way to a cover of "Footloose," and we rejoin Mama and the girls, who are holding court at a card table on the north side of the dance floor.

"Good heavens," says Gilda. "I thought I was going to have to hose you two down out there."

I glance at Mama, but she just smiles and raises her empty cup to us.

"I think someone needs a refill," Max says. "What are you drinking, Tess?"

"Beer—whatever they're serving in that keg over yonder."

Lonnie Sue drains the last from her plastic cup. "Oh, me, too. Max, would you be a sweetheart?"

"How about if I just get us all another round?"

Five pair of eyes watch him as he walks away.

"*Mmm-mmm*, that's my kind of man," Lonnie Sue purrs.

"Which one?" quips Dani. "From where I'm standing I

can see at least three that you're currently dating and five more you threw away."

Lonnie Sue feigns a glare at her.

I'm so glad that things are back to normal between them.

Dani clears her throat. "Well, now that we're all together, I have some news."

She hasn't said a word about Tommy since that day in the salon when Lonnie Sue delivered Sid's report. Dani and Renie spent a couple of nights at Mama's. Then with the help of Sid, she went home and kicked Tommy out. After Sid threatened to sic the Cocoa Beach vice squad on Lola, he went without much of a fuss.

I brace myself. I can't imagine that she's going to tell us that she took him back despite everything. I want to tell her it's not easy to be on your own, but she deserves better than that.

"First I want to say that y'all have always been like family to me. I don't know how I would've gotten through half of what I've been through without y'all. Tess, you've been especially kind to me, but... Oh, I'm just going to up and say it. I'm giving you notice that I'm quitting."

We all stare at her. I, for one, wonder if I heard her right or if maybe the loud music made it sound like she was giving her notice.

"What in heaven's name are you talking about?" Mama says, looking particularly stunned.

Dani smiles. "Let me finish. It's not for more than three

months yet. Not 'til Renie graduates in June. She just got a scholarship to Florida Atlantic University down in Fort Lauderdale, and, well, when she goes, I'm moving down there, too. I've filed for divorce from Tommy."

If we were stunned before, we're slack-jawed and speechless now.

"I'm moving to Miami. That way I'll be close to Renie—but not too close."

"Oh, you precious girl. Come here and let me hug your neck." Mama lurches forward and grabs a hold of Dani, who, I just noticed, is blinking back tears.

"I've never done anything like this in my life." She sniffs. "Never really traveled outside of this area. I mean, it's not Hollywood, Avril, but to me it's a big step. I've got to get out of here. I just can't breathe this air anymore."

I touch her arm. "Hollywood is not all it's cracked up to be. I am so proud of you for making this decision. It must have been so hard on you."

Dani shrugs. "Not really. I just got to a point where enough was enough. Renie's the one who helped me decide that. Not directly, of course, but she made me realize I want more for her than an unfaithful, cheating husband. I want her to know she deserves more than that and the best way I can show her that is by my actions."

The singer wails, "Everybody cut footloose." It could be the theme song of the night.

"I was thinking the other night that whether I know it or not, I may have waited until my daughter grew up to claim my own life. But she's worth it. If I never do anything else notable, I know I raised her and now I just want to make sure I keep doing right by her. I guess you might say she saved me. Even though it didn't seem like it when I found out I was pregnant in high school. Having that child was the best thing that ever happened to me."

"Kids will do that," Gilda says. "More than anything, they'll change your life."

CHAPTER 21

It's amazing the resilience of the human soul, how the will to be happy transcends even after fate has proven herself to be stone-cold and unfeeling—especially when you start believing you can be happy again.

The next morning started out that way—Max awakened me with a kiss and we made love before he left to attend to some business in Kissimmee. He asked if I wanted to go with him, but I declined so I could get a few things done around the house. We made plans to meet in his neck of the woods for a late lunch.

I'm just getting out of the shower when the phone rings.

"Avril, it's Zane."

Kally's Surfer Boy.

"Hi, Zane. What's up?"

I'm half expecting him to ask me if I can take Sam for a couple of hours, and reflexively, I glance around to make sure I've picked up all the condom wrappers.

"Kally's in the hospital."

I drop down onto the side of the bed, stunned because

she'd improved so much after being so sick that day we sprinkled Chet's ashes.

"What's wrong? Is she okay?"

There's a long pause on the other end of the line.

"Zane?"

"Yeah, I'm here. It's pneumonia. I had to take her to the emergency room last night because she was having a hard time breathing. She's in intensive care."

I press my hand to my heart, trying to stop its thudding. No. This can't be happening. She was getting better. She sounded better all those times I called.

"Can you come?" he asks. "She's at Cape Canaveral Hospital."

I'm already stepping into my clothes. "Of course. I'm leaving right now."

I CALL MAMA AND MAX before I leave for the hospital. Max offers to drop everything and come, but I tell him no, to finish his work, that it's best for me to go to the hospital alone.

"I'm here if you need me," he says. "You just call and I'll be right there."

As I drive I can't help think how very little preempted Chet's work. Sure, he came home for Kally when Caro died, but the funeral just happened to fall between shoots. Maybe I'm not being fair. Chet and I never faced any life-or-death situations together, unless you count the slow death of

NANCY ROBARDS THOMPSON   265

our marriage from him being gone so much and so caught
up in the show business machine. I don't know, maybe he
would've dropped everything like Max has offered.

I suppose I'll never know, but it feels good, comforting
to know that all I have to do is say the word and Max will
be here.

Mama's in the intensive care waiting room with Zane and
Sam when I get there. Sam's sleeping in her arms.

"Poor little fella's been here since the middle of the
night," Mama says. "Since they'll only allow two people in
with Kally at a time, I'll take him to my house so he can
stretch out and be comfortable."

Zane nods. "Thanks, Kally will appreciate it."

Zane looks worn out, sitting there with his elbows braced
on his knees, worry lines etched into his tan face. He buries
his face in his hands for a moment, then completes the
motion, running his hands through his shaggy blond hair.

Mama stands with Sam, but the boy doesn't even stir. She
pats his leg, gazing down at him. In that instant, I glimpse
the kind of grandmother she would've been. The kind of
Grammy who'd make a child so happy he fell asleep in her
arms, the kind who'd spoil a child mercilessly and bake
cookies and have special Grammy-and-me days.

And all that unspent love she has to share nearly
breaks my heart.

"Don't you worry about us. We'll be just fine." She

starts to walk, but hesitates, her brow knitting as she blinks back tears. "When y'all go in to see Kally, you tell her I love her, okay?"

Tears well in Mama's eyes as she hurries past us out into the hall.

"Mama, wait." I rush after her and give her my door key. "Here, take Sam home."

After they leave, Zane and I have to wait for the nurse to finish a procedure before we can go in and see Kally.

"I love her," Zane murmurs. "I could've made her and Sam happy if she would've let me."

A big tear meanders down his cheek and he makes no apologies or attempt to brush it away.

"Maybe if she'd let me she wouldn't be here right now."

He buries his face in his hands again and sobs.

"Sometimes—" My voice breaks. I clear my throat and close my eyes for a moment to gather my composure.

"I know you want to believe that," I finally say. "But sometimes all the love in the world can't change the course of fate."

Zane sobs and I don't even know if he hears me. But maybe the words weren't meant for him. Maybe they were meant for me.

KALLY'S HOOKED UP TO tubes and monitors and a ventilator. As I edge closer to her bedside, surreal images fly at me as if from a nightmare. One minute the sight of her lying there so still and frail under all that clicking and wheezing machinery nearly doubles me over in grief; the next minute the nurse's whisper reverberates in my ear. "You can't light that candle in here." She points to my hands.

I realize I'm clutching the red candle Kally brought that night we had dinner—back when it seemed as if our relationship was too torn to mend and that we had all the time in the world. But now I know better.

Strange, I barely remember grabbing the candle as I ran around the house, unable to get out of my own way, so I could get out the door and drive to the hospital.

In slow motion, the nurse reaches for the candle, but I clutch it to my chest.

"I won't light it. I promise. But she *needs* to see it. She needs to see that there's still a whole candle left to burn when she gets out of here."

The nurse looks unconvinced.

"Look, I don't have any matches or a lighter. This is for *after* she gets out of here. She *is* going to get well and seeing this will help her."

As the nurse fades into the background, she makes a *tsking* sound full of pity that seems to echo through the room. I hope Kally doesn't hear her because she would hate it.

That thought alone helps me refocus.

As if she senses me, Kally opens her eyes and flutters her fingers in greeting.

"Shhhhh." I smooth the hair off her forehead. "Save your strength so you can get well."

She closes her eyes, too weak to protest.

"She can't talk because of the ventilator," Zane says. "And they have her pretty heavily drugged."

I hold her hand, gently stroking her paper-thin skin with my thumb.

Suddenly, Kally's eyes fly open wide and she pulls out of my grasp and makes a jerky motion with her hand.

I stand there stupidly looking around trying to figure out what she wants, wondering if I should call the nurse. But Zane picks up a small dry erase board and marker off the bedside table and holds the board so she can write, *Sam* in big shaky letters.

"Don't worry," I assure her. "Mama has him. He's fine."

I hear the words as if someone else is uttering them, a stoic devoid of emotion, because I know if I let one iota of feeling seep through the cracks, I'll crumble and be swept into a sea of panic.

Underneath the word *Sam*, Kally writes, *Will U care 4 him?*

"You know I will, but we'll talk about that later. After you're out of here. You're *going to* get better, Kally."

She's writing again, long sloppy strokes that run off the board.

4 give me?

"Yes, absolutely. Oh, and look—" I hold out the candle.

"We have a lot of candle left to burn, a lot of catching up to do. So you have to get well so we can get to it."

The pen falls from her hand, and she looks at me with so much love in her tired eyes.

A single tear breaks free, and as I swipe it away, she tries to say something.

It comes out as a series of faint gurgles, but it sounds like, "I love you."

"I love you, too, my friend, my sister. Always have and always will."

She closes her eyes and drifts off to sleep.

Kally died a year ago today.

I never believed she'd go. Couldn't grasp it. Chet's passing was so sudden, as if he didn't have a choice. Kally's death was like watching the light and color gradually fade from the sky.

In the weeks following her death, I couldn't understand how the sun could rise. How the tide could turn. How the sky could be so damn blue.

I mean the light was gone. How was this possible?

Looking back, the memories of the two days she lingered are like a series of bright flashes and distorted clips from a bizarre movie—first I'm begging her to *hold on, just hold on a little longer. You can kick this thing. Sam needs you. I need you, Kally. Don't do this to me.*

In the end, the gravelly rattle of her breathing seemed to say, *Just this once it isn't about you, Av.* As if proving that point, the scene flashes to the doctor waving Kally's living will.

Why are you giving up on her so easily? Is this what you really want, Kally? How could you know when you were signing that piece of paper? Can't you just hold on a little longer? But she can't speak with the vent in her throat...she can't even write on her white board...she has no quality of life here... they click off the machines...eerie silence envelops us... her body shutters as she draws her final raspy breath...time of death—11:32 a.m.

We bury her in the Sago Beach Cemetery—the same place where we used to roller skate, where she eventually lost her virginity to Jake Brumly—in the shade of a prolific orange tree.

She'd already made the arrangements, except for clothing. I chose a blue dress for her. Her favorite color. The whole of Sago Beach turned out to pay their respects. The hypocrites. Where were they when she needed them?

I was devastated, and if not for Sam and Max, I would've had an even harder time coping. Blindly, as if I was a puppet guided by an unseen hand, I focused all my energy on those two, until finally one day I broke through the other side of the pain.

Today, one year later, Max and I have brought Sam to the cemetery to put flowers on her grave.

Has it really been a year? So much has changed.

Kally left Zane Lady Marmalade's, and he's running it as if she were still working beside him.

Dani made good on her promise and when the divorce was final—just after Renie graduated—she packed up and moved to Miami. She's working toward opening a salon in South Beach.

Lonnie Sue is still Lonnie Sue. Still chasing Sid and probably wouldn't know what to do if someday he lets her catch him. Though, I suspect someday he will, in fact, do just that.

Mama and Gilda are still holding court at the salon. I think Sago Beach would slide off into the ocean without them.

As for Max and me—we got married six months ago and we've adopted Sam as our own. Now, Max is the one officially in charge of baiting all hooks. He seems pretty thrilled with that position.

Sam has his moments when he misses his mother. We all do. But for the most part, we're a happy little family, the three of us—and the dog. And we're about to grow by one more.

I'm pregnant. About four and a half months along. The doctor says I'm past the danger zone, but he's monitoring me closely since I'm considered high-risk.

I don't know how, but I know in my bones this miracle baby will be born healthy and strong. Call it intuition—or call it fate. Call it whatever you want. All I know is I had to go full circle—cross-country into the hell of Hollywood and back to finally find my place in this world. Just like in the movies, I found it right here in my own backyard.

I don't regret my life with Chet. I wouldn't be who I am

today if not for him. The good and the bad, the growing and changing, has molded me into a stronger person.

A person who is whole.

A person who is content to live in a house in Sago Beach with a wonderful man and work in her mama's salon.

A person who knows that usually what glitters is only fool's gold. At least that's what they use in the movies.

As the final credits roll, Max holds up Sam so that he can pick an orange off the tree that shades his mama's grave.

As I watch them—my husband and son—I whisper a prayer of thanks that fate led me home. Maybe happily ever after doesn't only happen in the movies.

* * * * *

Turn the page for a sneak preview
of Kate Austin's riveting new title from NEXT,
SEEING IS BELIEVING,
coming to stores in October 2007.

I don't know what to expect, but I'm ready.

When the doorbell rings, I'm sitting in my office, hands on my lap, ready for whoever it is. I have known since noon that I must get organized because… Because why? I have never before anticipated something or someone's arrival.

There are two men at my door, one tall and broad, the other as close as can be to average without being a caricature of it.

"Ms. Sterling?" the tall one asks. "I'm Detective Jones. This is Detective Morrison." Jones gestures at Mr. Average.

Morrison holds out his photograph. This time I try to turn my head away but it's too late.

I have learned to conquer the rush of tears and nausea that comes with the gift, but the strength of the feeling always takes my breath away.

"Ms. Sterling?" Carrick Jones lightly touches my shoulder. "Are you all right?"

I shrug away from him. Cops are at once incredibly perceptive and blind. They know you're lying—for them, everyone is always lying—but not why. Good.

"I'm fine. Come in and tell me what you want."

I force myself to sit down quietly and wait. The authorities will not like me. Anyone who predicts death must be suspect in some way. So I wait, inwardly in turmoil, outwardly calm. I will *not* speak first.

The silence stretches until I am within a single moment of breaking it. I open my mouth to speak, but Jones beats me to it.

"You are Ria Sterling, aren't you?"

I wonder if he wants to see some identification or if I am not what he expects. A crone? A gypsy? Someone older or younger?

"Yes," I say.

"Do you recognize this woman?"

I hold the photograph gripped tightly in my hand but don't look. I hate cameras and I hate their product. I don't have a single photo in my house. I have paintings of my family on the walls and a silhouette, drawn from memory, of Mama Amata on my bedside table.

"Open your eyes."

The voice is gentle but it is an order, not a request. I refuse it.

"Do you know what I do?" I ask, my eyes squeezed shut. "Do you understand what you're asking? I see death," I begin, using words I've spoken a thousand times. "Somehow I see people's deaths in their photographs."

I brace myself for the shock and look down at the picture in my hands. Nothing happens. I rub my thumb over the woman's face. She looks familiar and for a moment I think I must know her, but I don't. I have, though, seen her face on the news. She's missing. Her name is...

"Lisa Alison Martin. She's been missing for two days."

I hold up my hand.

"I know who she is. But the photo says nothing to me."

I don't say what this most probably means—that Lisa Alison Martin is already dead. Instead I say again, "Nothing. It means nothing to me."

"Of course it doesn't." The sarcasm drops from Jones's mouth like acid. "Why would it? It's all a game to you, isn't it? Suckering all those poor schmucks who come to you for help, ripping them off while they're in pain.

"Come on, Morrison, let's get the hell out of here."

I scribble frantically on a piece of paper on my desk. I don't know why I want Carrick Jones to believe me but it's important. I put his name on an envelope and seal it.

"Take this. But don't open it until Monday."

I'm not sure whether he'll do what I ask nor what the cost of this action will be, but it's necessary. He takes the envelope and shoves it into his pocket.

"Thank you, Ms. Sterling, for nothing."

I take care not to touch Morrison as I follow the two of them to the door. Even without touch, a wave of sorrow rolls over me. I can't tell if it's him or me, but it's strong. I stumble and fall against him.

"Oh my God." I crumple to the floor, curling myself into a ball to get away from him. "Oh my God. Oh. Oh. Oh."

The agony is relentless, affecting every part of my body. My head throbs, my heart pounds.

"Call 9-1-1. Now."

I hear Carrick Jones through the haze of pain. And then everything and everyone vanishes.

TV journalist Charlie McNally is about to snag the scoop of a lifetime—proving a confessed murderer's innocence. Through all this Charlie has to juggle the needs of her professor boyfriend and his little girl, face time with her pushy mom who just blew into town—and face a deadly confrontation with the real killer....

Look for

Face Time

by

Hank Phillippi Ryan

Emmy® Award-winning
television reporter

Available October
wherever you buy books.

HARLEQUIN®
Next™

www.TheNextNovel.com

HARLEQUIN®
Super Romance®

*Welcome to our newest miniseries, about five
poker players and the women who love them!*

Texas Hold'em

When it comes to love, the stakes are high

Beginning October 2007 with

THE BABY GAMBLE

by USA TODAY *bestselling author*

Tara Taylor Quinn

#1446

Desperate to have a baby, Annie Kincaid
turns to the only man she trusts, her ex-husband,
Blake Smith, and asks him to father her child.

Also watch for:

BETTING ON SANTA *by Debra Salonen* November 2007
GOING FOR BROKE *by Linda Style* December 2007
DEAL ME IN *by Cynthia Thomason* January 2008
TEXAS BLUFF *by Linda Warren* February 2008

Look for THE BABY GAMBLE *by* USA TODAY
bestselling author Tara Taylor Quinn.

Available October 2007 wherever you buy books.

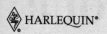

HARLEQUIN®

EVERLASTING LOVE™

Every great love has a story to tell™

An uplifting story of love and survival that spans generations.

Hayden MacNulty and Brian Conway both lived on Briar Hill Road their whole lives. As children they were destined to meet, but as a couple Hayden and Brian have much to overcome before romance ultimately flourishes.

Look for

The House on Briar Hill Road

by award-winning author
Holly Jacobs

Available October wherever you buy books.

www.eHarlequin.com

HEL65419

REQUEST YOUR FREE BOOKS!

2 FREE NOVELS PLUS 2 FREE GIFTS!

There's the life you planned. And there's what comes next.

NEXT07R

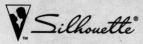

Romantic
SUSPENSE

**Sparked by Danger,
Fueled by Passion.**

When evidence is found that Mallory Dawes
intends to sell the personal financial information
of government employees to "the Russian,"
OMEGA engages undercover agent Cutter Smith.
Tailing her all the way to France, Cutter is
fighting a growing attraction to Mallory while at
the same time having to determine her connection
to "the Russian." Is Mallory really the mouse in
this game of cat and mouse?

Look for

Stranded with a Spy

by *USA TODAY* bestselling author

Merline Lovelace

October 2007.

Also available October wherever you buy books:

BULLETPROOF MARRIAGE *(Mission: Impassioned)*
by Karen Whiddon

A HERO'S REDEMPTION *(Haven)* by Suzanne McMinn

TOUCHED BY FIRE by Elizabeth Sinclair

HARLEQUIN®

Mediterranean
N I G H T S™

Sail aboard the luxurious Alexandra's Dream and
experience glamour, romance, mystery and revenge!

Coming in October 2007...

AN AFFAIR TO REMEMBER

by
Karen Kendall

When Captain Nikolas Pappas first fell in love with
Helena Stamos, he was a penniless deckhand and she
was the daughter of a shipping magnate. But he's
never forgiven himself for the way he left her—and
fifteen years later, he's determined to win her back.

Though the attraction is still there, Helena is hesitant
to get involved. Nick left her once...what's to stop
him from doing it again?

Ria Sterling has the gift—or is it a curse?—
of seeing a person's future in his or her
photograph. Unfortunately, when detective
Carrick Jones brings her a missing person's
case, she glimpses his partner's ID—and
sees imminent murder. And when her vision
comes true, Ria becomes the prime suspect.
Carrick isn't convinced this beautiful woman
committed the crime...but does he believe
she has the special powers to solve it?

Look for

Seeing Is Believing

by

Kate Austin

Available October
wherever you buy books.

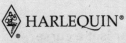

HARLEQUIN®

COMING NEXT MONTH

#93 FACE TIME • Hank Phillippi Ryan

TV journalist Charlie McNally's reporting is about to prove
a confessed murderer's innocence and set her free. But just
as she's snagging the scoop of a lifetime, Charlie's mother
hits town for a little plastic surgery. Now Charlie has to
juggle the needs of her professor boyfriend and his little girl,
as well as face time with her pushy mom—and brave
a deadly face-off with the real killer....

#94 SEEING IS BELIEVING • Kate Austin

Ria Sterling has the gift—or is it a curse?—of seeing a
person's future in his or her photograph. Unfortunately,
when detective Carrick Jones brings her a missing person's
case, she glimpses his partner's ID—and sees imminent
murder. And when her vision comes true, Ria becomes the
prime suspect. Carrick isn't convinced this beautiful woman
committed the crime...but does he believe she has the
special powers to solve it?